LUCA

OR LUCA

LUNA NOVELLA #11

www.lunapresspublishing.com
ISBN-13: 978-1-913387-87-7.

To my mom.
Thank you for giving me this life,
and later on - for saving it.

Content Warning: Self-harm.

Contents

1. Luca

Luca opens her eyes to the unbearable brightness of the sun seeping in through her open window. A shy gust of wind flirtatiously tickles her face as she sits up in her bed. It's too much to handle. Everything is.

Compromised, she drops her head back onto her mustard pillow and lifts her butterfly blanket up to the very tip of her nostrils. She takes in a deep breath through her nose, filling herself with warm air smelling of her body odour and the strangely comforting smell of freshly washed sheets.

You gotta get up, she thinks (says) to herself.

She had always spoken to herself. She was never alarmed by the voices inside her, not even the ones she could barely control.

After around thirty minutes of staring at her egg-coloured ceiling, Luca finally sits up in her bed; time for take two. Her room is flooded with light; she can't help but choke on it. While squinting, she flings her butterfly blanket off her young body and gets out of bed in a quick motion. She ignores the little black dots that come creeping in from the corners of her vision and opens the bedroom door. She walks down the empty hall to the bathroom that she shares with her older sister. There, she takes a shower, trying to keep it short in order to avoid the cluster of thoughts in her head, threatening to pile up until her brain is filled to the brim – threatening to explode.

She gets out of the shower and dries herself off, yet her feet feel awfully wet, so she violently drags them across the soaked bathmat – seeming only to wet them even further. Frustrated, she walks out of the bathroom with a towel wrapped around her body and goes into her room to dress. She leaves a slimy trail of youth behind her, like a snail in the winter. Back in her room, she gets dressed in the usual oversized jacket and mom jeans. Never tights – god forbid – those things require a full commitment to the shape of your body.

"Luca! Are you coming to eat breakfast!?" her sister screams from the kitchen.

Luca only rolls her eyes instinctively. Then, she mindlessly puts on a pair of socks over her dripping feet and makes her way towards the kitchen.

Breakfast is filled with words and bowls of cereal not worth mentioning. Only her sister and herself – the way it always is – and as soon as she manages to cut herself loose from her sister's attention, she slips out the door and goes straight to her bike.

Her eyes melt into her heart when she sees them leaning elegantly on the streetlamp, exactly where she had left them the night before.

She loves her bike. She loves them because they're hers. It's only two wheels connected by metal, coloured with fuchsia and dust, but somewhere in between the wheels and the handgrips lies her independence. Somewhere in between the faded fuchsia and the high seat lives her freedom.

She bikes fast. Always fast. She's not content until she's taken aback by her speed, until her heart skips a beat. In that lost beat lies her excitement – which up until that moment had been dormant deep between her ribs. She loves the aerial resistance under her chin that lifts her face up to the clouds. She loves the wind that blows her headache deep into oblivion… because otherwise her head always hurts.

She always hurts.

After passing through practically the entire city of Telo – 'the heart of the Middle East' – she arrives at a strange street, with an overwhelming atmosphere of familiarity. Deja Vu, she says to herself.

She stands in front of the apartment building labelled Juvo 16, feeling around with her eyes, searching for a floating scrap of bravery waiting to be snatched. The air seems unusually clear, so she gives up and instead walks up to the intercom and presses the number 2. Nothing happens. She's about to press again when an alarmingly loud buzz slips out of the intercom. She pushes the door forward and the door 'clicks' in agreement.

Luca starts walking up a flight of dusty stone stairs until she sees a door with the number 2 proudly stuck to it. She's about to knock when she realises that the door is slightly opened already. She pushes the door slowly, cautiously steps inside and says, "Hello?"

No one answers, so she starts inspecting her surroundings. She's surprised by how ridiculously obvious she finds this new space to be. White, sterile walls perfectly accommodate the plastic fumes whistling out of the spotless air conditioner hanging on the west wall. A black counter stands underneath the spewing air conditioner. On the counter is a coffee machine, and a cooler with a neat pile of plastic cups stacked beside it. Of course, there's also the mandatory glass candy jar filled with many colourful, unrelated types of hard candy that look barely edible. Hiding behind the candy jar Luca notices a white noise machine, and for the first time since she's entered the room, she hears that it's filling the small (yet uncomfortably barren) room with 'soothing' ocean sounds.

I fucking hate therapists, she (screams) says to herself.

Suddenly, a door in front of her opens alarmingly slowly, as if she were a sleeping beast someone was afraid to awake. Honestly, she didn't even notice that there was a door in the wall in front of her. Previously the door was completely swallowed by the overwhelming whiteness of the room.

A short woman made of porcelain comes out from behind the door. Her dark brown hair is slicked back into a ponytail, and an oversized grey dress hangs from her bony shoulders. She cracks a large, robotic smile and Luca swears she can hear a metallic squeak as the outer corners of her lips draw upwards.

"Hello," the porcelain woman says gently. "Luca?"

"Yes," Luca answers shortly.

"Come on in." She gestures for her to come into this even newer space.

Luca sits down on a beige comforter and the porcelain woman places herself in an identical one positioned in front of her own. There's a large overhead picture of Telo's coastline hung on the wall behind the woman's head. Luca tries to locate her house within the buildings running alongside Telo's beachy strip when suddenly she realises that the porcelain woman has been speaking. "...So that's a little bit about me." Ms. Porcelain pauses but quickly continues, "It's nice to finally meet you."

"Yeah," Luca answers shortly and looks down at her shoes. Her baby blue sneakers are peppered with wet patches.

What the hell is up with my feet??

"Tell me a little bit about yourself." Ms. Porcelain cuts off the voice in her head.

Luca spurts out her usual synopsis, with only the one change of an updated number. "I'm 17. I dropped out of school. You're my fifth psychologist in the last year."

And now there's silence. There's no mistaking it.

Luca looks down at her feet once again. The wet patches are gone. Now the entire shoe is soaked to the brim. This once baby blue sneaker is now a royal blue soaking wet mess.

"I can see that this is hard for you," Ms. Porcelain points out. An observant little machine.

"Yeah. I'm tired," Luca excuses dully.

Luca is beyond annoyed… her body is twitching, trying to shake off the feeling as if it were a tick.

After the appointment is over and Luca is back on her bike, she speeds through the streets in hope that the wind will tear off the burdening weight of the last hour. She waits for the magic. She still believes in it. Isn't that enough reason for magic to exist?

*

Ms. Porcelain's words are floating around the septic room; they're unbelievably bleak, and barely audible. Luca looks around at the white walls, trying to find something she hadn't noticed before. It's strange how in these drab, empty clinics, she happens to find the most extreme amount of detail — while in normally accessorised rooms there seems to be a bigger picture that numbs her refined observation skills.

Luca finds a square inch of undone stitches in the off-white carpet under their feet. She notices a spotless tin trashcan standing in the corner of the room, reflecting off the light seeping in through the curtain. She steals a glance at an old coffee stain on the curtain. There's the overhead picture of Telo with a tan frame, and a small wooden desk on the carpet between herself and Ms. Porcelain. On the desk is a cream-coloured clock and a tissue box with a tired floral print.

Only when she tunes in to the sounds does she hear the silence.

She doesn't know what she's supposed to say.

"I don't know what I'm supposed to say," Luca says.

"Just tell me how you've been," Ms. Porcelain answers simply.

Silence.

"Just tell me how you've been feeling this last week."

"Tired," Luca answers finally.

"Uh-hm," is the answer

Throw me a bone here!

"Just feeling empty and hopeless," Luca says, and it takes up all of the energy that she can muster.

"Yeah. Why do you feel hopeless?"

This is hopeless.

"I just feel like I have no future."

"Why do you feel that?"

I'm going to kill her.

"Because I can barely do simple things. Like brushing my teeth."

"I see," Ms. Porcelain says. And then, "Do you want to get better?"

That useless piece of –

Huh. I actually don't want to get better.

2. Dani

"Ladies and gentlemen, as we start our descent, please make sure your seat backs and tray tables are in their full upright position. Make sure your seat belt is securely fastened and all carry-on luggage is stowed underneath the seat in front of you or in the overhead bins. Thank you."

Dani allows her forehead to drop to the oval window beside her, her eyes looking out at Telo's coastline spread out in front of her, looking like spilled soda foaming on a sandy yellow countertop. Dani keeps her gaze pinned on the coastline as the plane gently moves forward and downwards into the clouds. Her thoughts swiftly jump into the view.

Why the hell did we travel all that way? she thinks to herself, Why did we spend all that money to go to a place resembling home, and why was it ever so lovely and new? Why did we love spending time on an imposter beach in a foreign land, with its mocking similarities and outrageously expensive sunscreen?? Why did we choose to travel to a place like home?

Then, in order to supply quick relief to her poking wonderings, she searches within herself for an answer. It hurts, the doubts poking all around, but at last she settles on: I guess even our sense of wonder has its limits. Perhaps we can only imagine what we' ve already seen.

She turns to look over at Dawn, who's laying on her right shoulder and snoring ever so lightly.

We sure are a strange pair, she thinks to herself. Yet Dani has no idea what strange is, or what strange really does. Not yet, at least.

Dani finds it hard to believe that all the people in Telo had kept on living their lives without her presence. How is it possible that while she was all the way across the world, everyone back home kept on existing? Of course, she knew that most people were unaware of her existence, and yet it felt incredibly strange that they would be so entirely disconnected from her. It's simply too hard to believe that while she was laying on a beach on the other side of the world some housewife all the way back here in the Middle East was doing laundry, or cooking dinner. Didn't people cease to exist once she wasn't looking?

*

Dani and Dawn land at Soncubion airport. It's a relatively modern building with faux granite everything. Yet there's a magic to it, like every airport in the world; the magic of a place leading to all places. Dani has always loved airports. She loves to think of them as a place that stops time and loosens the concept of location. Whenever in airports, she feels as if she's nowhere – with everywhere to go. Yet the magic of airports only lasts for as long as you stay inside its walls. The second you step outside you're irreversibly stuck inside the reality of your current location.

In Dani and Dawn's case, the reality outside of Soncubion Airport is the dense summer air of the Middle East. There's no escape from its humidity, and its nature is too thick to allow even a small gust of wind to break through its dictating existence.

Dani looks up at Dawn, who's standing beside her, his long scrawny arms stretched down to his suitcase handle. His face is covered almost entirely in pearls. All kinds of pearls; silvery-white, dark purple, and lazy pink all over his face. Real, round, three-dimensional pearls. Why in the hell does he have pearls on his face?

Then the realisation drops, sharp and clear in her mind.

Pearls of sweat. That's how the saying goes.

Dawn feels her eyes grazing his face, so he looks down into the big brown planets she claims to see through. His face is giving into his confusion.

"I'm sweating like a pig. I can't stop thinking about how disgusting I must be," he says.

"Yeah," Dani says softly, and then a bit more reassuringly, "yeah, I wouldn't worry too much about how you look if I was you. I would be more worried about that smell – man..."

They smile at each other and laugh. Their smiles alone are the gust of wind that will never come. Things have always looked up for Dani when Dawn is happy. Things are always better when Dawn smiles. Things always seem brighter whenever there's the joyous presence of another; our world is coloured only as bright as the smile beside us. After all, it's through the happiness of others that we find our own.

*

They find their way home in a hell shaped like a taxi, filled to the brim with cigarette smoke and a driver that won't stop staring at Dani's chest through the overhead mirror. Dani lifts up the collar of her shirt, and simultaneously sends out a signalling cough, yet the driver keeps staring at her chest, dodging all the clues. His stares sting, but it's his imagination that stinks up the entire cab.

Eventually, exhausted by Dani's suppressed silence, Dawn lifts both arms and cups Dani's breasts. He gives them two hearty squeezes. Dani explodes with laughter, but the driver seems less amused. He looks at the young friends from within his overhead mirror, and his eyes open wide with surprise – an instinct which is quickly followed by the incredibly conscious decision of scrunching his nose, a gesture infused with disgust. Dani can see the driver's face turn a murky green; a real, vile green. Dawn doesn't seem to notice.

Both of them get out of the taxi at Dawn's house.

The second the taxi drives out of view Dawn blurts out, "Oh my god, I bet that bloated asshole eats microwaved sandwiches, watches reruns of 'Trailer Park Boys' and beats his wife late at night."

"Don't joke about that," Dani says. She shoots him a stern look.

He shrugs as if to say, 'what are you gonna do about it, huh?' – a gesture Dani has long ago learned to despise in silence and cover with ignorance. Dawn quickly continues, "You gotta admit that he was one hell of a McDonald's loving, sexually unsatisfied, ketchup-stained-sports-t-shirt-wearing-son-of-a-bitch.”

Dani laughs in approval.

An hour later, both of them are strewn across Dawn's tiny yellow couch in front of the TV. They've both showered, and with their hair still dripping, they leave wet patches all across the couch, turning its uniform yellow skin into a desert of mustard spots.

Dani fights to keep her eyes open in spite of the jet lag. She looks around Dawn's one-bedroom apartment. It's shabby, yet comforting and warm. The egg-coloured walls are cracked and peeled, decorated with reflecting poster papers depicting movie scenes and book quotes. Besides the yellow couch, there's a maroon closet leaning at an alarming angle on one of the walls. There's a small kitchen with a few open cabinets revealing a small selection of pots and pans sized for meals of one, and multiple coloured plastic cups stacked on one another. A few feet to her right is a large window, seemingly holding up the ceiling with its wide sill. The window reveals the skin of the street; taupe apartment buildings marked with age, blooming fuchsia bushes lined before the entrance path to each building, cars parked tightly on both sides of the street and green streetlights with an alarming amount of bikes tied at their feet.

“Are you going to go back to live with your parents in Praeter?” Dawn asks with the voice of a man speaking through the shutter of a dream.

“I mean, all my stuff is still there. But I don't want to go back, you know?”

“Of course I know,” he chuckles. “That's why I moved out

of my parents' place ages ago."

"Yeah, I know. I just…" Dani pauses. "I just don't know what to do. Before we left, the trip was all I thought about. And now that we're back, I feel like I can't go back to living the same life. I mean, I'm 22 for fuck sake. I gotta start living my own life."

"I think I'm going to apply for University. I mean, maybe it's time I stop fucking around," Dawn says.

"I can't do that yet. I don't even know what I would want to study," Dani replies.

"So you don't want to go back to living at your parents' place, and you don't want to go study. What are you going to do? You gonna go back to work at the cafe? Aren't you sick of that already?"

"No, fuck that, I'm not going back to the cafe'. The cafe was for the trip and for the trip alone. Now I need some sort of job that includes housing, like… like an au pair."

"Dani, an au pair is someone who works overseas on a legal visa for a couple of years. But I guess you could be a full-time nanny or something like that."

It takes a few more minutes of talk, but eventually, Dawn says what she wants to hear. "You can stay here until you figure things out."

*

"You gotta get the hell out of here," Dawn says.

This hadn't come as much of a surprise to Dani. She had seen a wall begin to form between them the second she moved in. At first, it was so faint it was barely there – and yet she could see it. For Dani, these things have never been something she's sensed. Not at all, in fact – they were as real as rain on your skin, or perhaps, a slap in the face.

The wall between them kept creeping into solidity; at first, it was at small intervals, fifty shades of translucent. Then, one day, it began to heavily flirt with opaqueness.

Eventually, it was a brick wall through and through, and there was no going around it. This was no feeling; the wall was there. She could see it, alright.

Even so, she decides to use the 'baffled' approach.

"What??"

"I'm sorry, I just ca-n-n-ot anymore." Dawn puts both forefingers on his temples and closes his eyes.

"What? I haven't been a nuisance at all! I've only been sitting here watching TV for the past month!"

"Exactly! That's the only fucking thing you've been doing! I can't see you wasting away like some living corpse in front of my TV."

Dani's face shows no marks of remorse. And so, Dawn continues, "On my couch, in my own home, under my watch, under my roof, in mi casa – not su casa, under my care, under my watchful eye and aching heart, in my—"

"I get it, I get the point! But I've also been so helpful! I've been doing all the dishes and cooking us dinner, and even doing your laundry!"

"Yes! You're doing nothing, but you're also doing too much!"

The paradox doesn't escape his mind, and yet he's someone who knows all too well how to bury his words as well as brush away insecurities from his face and tone. He continues confidently, declaring courageously, "You're doing nothing for yourself, and too much for me!"

Dani rolls her eyes. Dawn realises that there's nothing left but the truth. "I mean, goddamnit! I just miss walking around naked in my own freaking home! I need to reclaim that right not only as a homeowner, but also as a man." His eyes are laughing – as they always are – and yet they're matte. She can see the dull ache of sincerity buried deep behind his murky pupils. Perhaps he is serious about this after all.

What a jerk.

"What am I supposed to do?" she asks.

Feeling defeated and stranded at a dead-end, Dani decides to call her mom. Mom will know what to do, won't she? It always seems to be the case, even when you're twenty-two. Perhaps that's one thing that will never change. Dani has long ago realised that her mom doesn't know everything, and yet her mom seems to know enough. Perhaps it's only her voice, or the never-ending stream of love, but either way mom's words always bring relief.

"Sweetie, why don't you go to gran'mas? I've been meaning to get her some help anyways. She's getting too old to be all by herself."

And that was that. Once the idea had sprouted in mom's mind, and intravenously entered Dani's ears, there was no escaping it. A prophecy was born.

*

The prophecy was coming to life all too quickly.

"But what's wrong with your grandma?" Dawn asks.

"My grandma is a freaking witch."

I hate the stuff I say when I'm with him…

Wait – Did I really just think that?

"What does that even mean?" Dawn almost manages to sound like he cares.

"She's just always been a little off. I don't know exactly why, or by how much, but she's definitely off. Besides, I haven't been to her house in like a decade. So now I'm just going to suddenly move in?"

"That's what you did with me."

Dani only exhales roughly and says, "This shit stinks."

"As shit does," Dawn intercepts.

You always need to get the last word in, don't you.

Dani can see the wall between them finally begin to fade away as the promise of her departure grows stronger. Once again, she can see his face through the muted bricks. She decides to take advantage of the moment.

"You know, sorry is as sorry does…" She tries one last time.

"I love you like a sister, but there's no way you're staying here any longer."

That was the end of an era. Feeling as brief as it honestly was, Dani couldn't quite conquer the fear that life is too damn fleeting. Every moment passes before she could capture it. She keeps trying to marinate in the now, yet tomorrow keeps coming too fast.

Meanwhile…

3. Luca

Luca feels as though every second bears the suffering of a lifetime. Every minute goes by in the shape of years.

She's sitting on the stone-cold floor of the shower, folded into herself. She watches the blood run from her wrist and into the drain.

She's showering, yet she feels like she's drowning.

Though she always is… the water falling on her bare back simply makes it more believable. More real.

She showers, but she also sins at the same time.

She watches her red river flow.

So alive.

So real.

So incredibly painful.

But I'm controlling it, she says to herself.

I'm the queen of this river.

I decide where it starts to flow.

I decide when it dries out.

I decide how much it takes from me.

She showers.

But she's really not showering at all. She uses no soap, she takes no notice of her hair. She simply sits under the steaming faucet with her blade.

"Luca! When are you coming out?? I need to shower as well, you know!" her sister yells from outside the bathroom door.

Luca can feel her sister's fury radiate into her bones. This supplies her with enough energy to stand up, turn off the water and get out of the shower. She grabs a small red sock she finds in the dirty clothes pile lying in the corner of the bathroom and takes it up to her wrist. She squeezes the sock long and hard over her cuts, waiting for the bleeding to stop.

"Luca, can you hear me? I NEED to shower as well!"

"ONE SECOND!!" Luca whips her with a scream. From then on, silence ensues inside and outside of the white bathroom door.

After a few minutes of pressing the red sock to her wrist, Luca tosses it back to the dirty clothes pile and wraps herself in a towel. She gets out of the bathroom and walks to her room, where she quickly begins to rummage around in her underwear drawer in search of the hidden box of band-Aids ('waterproof', as well as 'extra large'). She finds it and grabs a strip, undresses the band-aid from its plastic outerwear, and sticks it over her cut in one quick, proficient swipe. Then, she puts on her pyjamas, at first unaware of the fact that her pyjama top has short sleeves, exposing her reddened wrist. However, the realisation is quick to follow her heedlessness; she digs in her closet for a long-sleeved pyjama top and puts it on. Lastly, she crumples onto her bed and lays there feeling stiff and empty.

Some time passes. Perhaps seconds, maybe hours – probably minutes. Her yellow curls are browned by the water soaking inside them – only the tips of her locks are shining gold. She has one hand laying on her forehead acne, trapping a dim headache within her mind. The other hand is laying on her heart. She feels her heart beating, not from her chest but within her freshly cut wrist. She feels her skin pulsing with ache and exhaustion. It's comforting. She finally feels that she has a real reason to rest. A real reason to feel as bad and hurt as she does. A bloody distraction. A pain that not only can she feel, but also see and touch. She will have to take care of this cut now, for the next couple of days at least. She will get to see it heal and improve, and eventually fade into a scar. She will have the satisfaction of knowing that she fixed it all by herself. She handled it. *Her*.

"Luca?" She suddenly hears a timid voice from outside of her bedroom door.

Her heart jumps and so does she. Quickly, she checks to see if her wrist is covered by her sleeve. When she manages to even her breaths, she says as nonchalantly as possible, "Yeah, come in."

In comes her older sister. Her expression is apologetic, mixed with something else. Luca excuses it as weariness, yet someplace inside she knows it's the expression of a person approaching a wounded animal.

Her sister's appearance is so like her own; golden locks that fall over her breasts, a curvy waist, a pale face with tiny eyes, short legs and huge feet. The only difference is the acne. Her sister never had it, and probably never will. Her sister is lucky like that, as well as beautiful and smart, yet not too smart for her own good (as Luca is, and always had been).

"I booked you an appointment to see a psychiatrist."

Luca suddenly feels her limbs harden, and her blood runs cold.

"You did what?"

"I... It's just that your therapist called me. She was very nice, but she said that you need to see a psychiatrist. She's worried about you. And I am too! I see you jumping from therapist to therapist and never getting better... and by the way, it's practically using up all the money that dad sends us. If you even care. And... and you have this look in your eyes all the time like you're... like you're—"

"LIKE I'M WHAT??" Luca can't help but shout.

"Like you're dead," her sister says. "Like you're dead," she repeats.

"Get out," Luca says.

"Luc…"

"GET OUT!" she yells.

Her sister drops her eyes to the stone floor and slowly backs out of the room.

In turn, Luca drops her gaze and waits for the tears to come flowing down. She waits and waits, but they don't come. Overcome by anger, she pounds her fists onto her bed, one after the other, again and again, and again…. Until eventually she manages to squeeze out a soft cry from her lips in an attempt to invoke some tears. No success.

Suddenly – as if hypnotised – she stops hitting her mattress and simply sits on the edge of her bed, staring out of her window with an empty glance. Her pupils are skidding inside her iris, but she's not looking at anything in particular. She sees nothing, but her dead eyes could swallow the universe whole.

After a long while, she looks down at her feet. In a second, her emotionless gaze spreads wide in horror. She sees that her feet are wrinkled and pale, and that they've somehow been inserted into a deep cell of a clear liquid that goes up to her knees, defying gravity and any other earthly logic.

What the hell??

She drags her head down and sideways to view the lower part of her legs from the side. She blinks once. She blinks twice. She rubs her eyes hard. Yet nothing changes.

In front of her, she still sees her pale calves existing within this peculiar capsule of floating water that goes all the way down to her wrinkly feet.

I'm going crazy, she thinks to herself. *I've officially lost it.*

There seems to be an outer capsule; malleable, thin, and invisible, and when her finger comes in touch with it the clear layer wobbles slightly back and forth like jello.

Overcome by curiosity, Luca gets up and spreads her legs. The floating liquid splits in half between her thighs, yet it doesn't spill, it simply morphs into two separate cells that surround each lower leg. It looks as though she's wearing some type of futuristic, chrome, clear, knee-high socks. Her mind scattered, she tries to walk towards the desk standing below her window, but she finds it difficult to move with all the extra weight around her legs. She feels heavy and utterly exhausted when she reaches the table. There, she grabs a pair of scissors and uses them to try to poke at the clear capsule. Yet no matter how hard she stabs at it, it doesn't budge — it only jiggles around, wiggling violently like some child being tickled to a pulp.

Luca, feeling sick to her stomach, goes back to sit on her bed. She wants to call for her sister to come back, but holds herself from doing so. She sits up and takes deep breaths. In and out. In and out. In through the nose. Out through the mouth.

Out of the blue, an idea clicks within her mind. She picks up her phone and swiftly dials Ms. Porcelain's number. Ms. Porcelain may be useless, but she's all that she's got.

When she finally picks up, Luca immediately skips the customary 'hello' and says, "Can you meet me tomorrow?"

*

The next day Luca is flying through the streets atop her bike. The world is blurred all around her, and finally, she feels safe in her skin. She almost forgets about the hovering liquid around her lower legs.

She had found it quite difficult to put on shoes this morning, for the capsule goes all the way down and around her feet. At last, she had managed to squeeze her feet into an exceptionally worn-out sneaker, yet the liquid bulged and swelled all around the lip of the shoe.

Luca makes her way towards Juvo 16. When she gets there she ties her bike to the nearest pole, enters the building, goes up the stairs and into the clinic. Today Ms. Porcelain is wearing high-waisted dark denim pants, with a long-sleeved turtleneck tucked inside. Her shoes are flat yet formal. Her dark hair is slicked back into a ponytail, as it had been the first time they met.

They say their hellos. At first, Ms. Porcelain rummages

through questions, until she finds the needle of truth in the haystack. Not Luca's truth, but *a* truth that she can identify within her. The truth comes forward with the help of a push shaped like a question, "How much longer do you think you can keep on going like this?"

"Maybe I don't plan to," Luca answers instinctively, and immediately regrets it.

Luca doesn't bother looking up to see Ms. Porcelain's reaction – she is already worlds away. Yet, somehow, she's also all too aware of the thin layer of liquid around her legs.

She starts to imagine herself jumping into an ocean. She can already feel the water surrounding her body (since it's no leap from the truth). She starts to swim blindly forward, slicing through the salty haven. She swims deeper and deeper, or perhaps shallower and shallower – she has no way of knowing. With her eyes still shut, she's going to all places at once. She is going nowhere with the intention of going everywhere. She feels the intent burn deep inside her, and it's so refreshing, and necessary. *Finally*, she wants to get somewhere.

She slowly opens her eyes, and the salt seeping in burns her in a way that she has been waiting for her entire life. That's when she spies an unidentifiable figure up ahead. She effortlessly floats towards it, and almost bumps into it, but manages to stop at the last second. She quickly backs up by hitting the water with long strokes, and finally sees the entirety of what's in front of her. She can feel herself jump out of her skin. What she sees, she can't process, yet her eyes aren't wise enough to look away.

What she sees is herself, except this Luca isn't breathing. No bubbles are coming out of her nose, and her body is stiff.

Her eyes look lost and unresponsive – which makes them the only bodily feature left unchanged. The Luca in front of her is undeniably gone.

Luca doesn't know what to feel. She's as jealous as she is horrified by the scene in front of her.

I just thought I had more time, Luca thinks to herself. *How can I already be dead… I've only just realised that I'm numb. This can't be real.*

And sure enough, it isn't.

Ms. Porcelain and Luca have a long chat about Luca's lost childhood – yet somehow, Luca barely participates. Luca doesn't bring up the reason for setting up this unscheduled appointment. Even when Ms. Porcelain sticks her questions down Luca's throat, Luca still doesn't budge. She just keeps looking down at her calves, watching the liquid travel up and over her knees. The more they talk, the more she sinks into it. By the time they're done speaking, it has come all the way up to her eyes. She can barely breathe, and the world is coloured a bluish-grey. She inhales air and chokes on water, somehow all at the same time. Everything is blurry and far away. She's so disconnected from the world, she's barely a part of it.

*

When she bikes on her way back home, she can feel every one of her muscles fighting to move, struggling to find a reason to keep on going. Her breath is heavy, her face is warm and sweaty and her entire body is swimming in liquid. She can barely feel where her skin ends and the liquid begins. She's so heavy, so unbearably blue. She's so blue that she's every blue; ultramarine, azure, turquoise, midnight, indigo, berry... She's a dirty mix of them all, a colour of no name, a colour of no need.

When Luca gets back home, the change of lighting tricks her eyes into thinking that she can see clearly. Taking advantage of the moment, she walks straight to her sister's room, slams the door open without knocking and says, "I'll go to the psychiatrist."

She regrets it immediately. Her eyes become accustomed to the overhead lighting of the house, and she quickly comes to realise that her eyes are still swimming in distortion. She finds herself fishing for the girl inside her who had the need to seek help. She's nowhere to be found, yet she was there just a moment ago.

*

Luca and her older sister are sitting in the waiting room of the psychiatrist's office. Luca looks over at her sister – she seems so alike, yet somehow she's entirely someone else. Her sister is wearing an oversized army green coat with tight black overalls underneath. She has high heels, high tits and lips capable of a smile. Fuck her.

"Luca?" A woman comes out and asks.

Luca goes inside the room with the strange woman and tries to open up as much as she possibly can. It takes a lot of work pushing her voice through the layer of liquid. Her eyes keep wanting to shut.

Luca mentions nothing of the water surrounding the entirety of her body. Even so, she steps out of the room with a prescription.

*

"I harm myself," Luca answers outright. She doesn't find her self-harm to be quite that peculiar. It had become a routine, and an integral part of her survival. On the other hand, it had become harder to cut herself ever since her whole body was encapsulated by water. It takes more of her time and strength to cut through the layer of liquid. The liquid never pops, or rips; it simply feels like a hard surface in the way of her skin.

Ms. Porcelain is silent, and her face is unaffected, barely bothered, as if Luca had just been speaking about the weather.

Or, maybe, is that a tear in her eye?

Nope, just the overhead light swimming in the corners of her eyes.

People react more wildly when asked if they want a piece of gum, Luca thinks to herself.

"Do you ever think about ending your life?" Ms. Porcelain asks, without moving a muscle in her face.

What the hell… I might as well say…

"Yeah," Luca shoots out.

The room goes numb from silence. Luca forcibly shallows her breathing, in fear of disturbing the stillness. She hates sitting there on that tilted beige comforter – she hates it now more than ever. Her skin begins to itch as if breaking out in an allergic reaction to the dead air.

Eventually, Ms. Porcelain swings out the deadliest of weapons (her slick, barren voice) and shatters the iron curtain. "What do you do throughout the week? On the days that you don't come to speak with me?"

Luca takes in a deep breath, swallowing the air in hope

of it automatically shooting out words. Yet there's no mercy in this life. The air she breathes answers only with an exhale, filled with the hot mist of her lungs. She battles to speak. "I'm usually in bed. Watching videos on my laptop."

"What do you think about hospitalisation?" Ms. Porcelain says, and there's a new tone in her voice. Not a soothing one.

She literally doesn't know what to do with me.

Luca doesn't answer, even though her brain is filled with words running around wildly, forming sentences that even she can't understand.

The topic of hospitalisation never comes up again.

4. Dani

Dani walks up to the front gate of her grandma's house. Her mind is swimming, and her gaze burns through the rusty metal gate. Old memories suddenly seem to come into high-definition. She can remember coming to visit her grandma on multiple occasions, but she can only recount one time when she stayed the night. Through the memories, she tries to relive that night; she can remember her grandma – while in the process of making dinner – pulling out a plastic bag of frozen edamame from the fridge. She recalls the way her Gran had spilled the frozen shells into a pot filled with boiling water. The frozen edamame pods had looked so lifeless slipped inside their dusty shade of green, and to the touch – they had been as stiff as Legos. Yet miraculously, only 10 minutes later, her Gran had claimed that they were ready to eat. She had fished out the edamame with a strainer and put them all in a porcelain bowl adorned with small blue flowers that Gran had called 'forget-me-nots'. Dani had peered down into the bowl, looking at the bulging pods of edamame, coloured a lively green. Had they been that same colour before? She couldn't quite remember. 'Colours are a slippery detail in the eyes of memory," Gran had said. Dani had only nodded in response, not quite understanding the intent.

But now, as Dani's eyes focus back on what's in front of her, she starts to carefully inspect the rusty metal gate, sprinkled with peeling specks of fuchsia paint. She could almost swear that this gate had been coloured an ocean blue. Perhaps colour is a slippery little queen after all.

Dani lifts her forefinger, and with her nail peels off a small piece of paint. When she's done, she stares at the exposed metal bones of the gate. As surprising as it may seem, no feelings emerge from the sight.

She's simply putting off the inevitable. She needs to go inside. They had scheduled for her to come at 11 am, and the time is already 11:15, with seemingly no intent to stop there.

Come on girlie, just go, she tells herself.

The voice in her mind supplies movement to her feet and direction to her walk. In seconds, she's past the metal gate and walking up the pathway to the front door. She walks under the arched doorway and buzzes the number 3 on the intercom.

"Shit, that's not the right one," she says.

Because of course it's not – the right apartment is number 2.

Next thing, she's knocking on the front door of the apartment, and her Gran opens the door.

"My darling! Oh, I haven't seen you in years!"

"Hey Gran," Dani says and leans down to give her a hug. "But I'm pretty sure I saw you a month ago when we had dinner at mom's."

"Years, I tell you! Years!" is her gran's reply.

Dani simply tightens her lips together and nods politely.

Gran turns her back to Dani, walking back into the small

apartment. She gestures for Dani to come inside, then tugs on her dusty black dress. While pulling a suitcase behind her, Dani steps inside and trails behind her Gran. She looks around. It's been years since she's come over – perhaps even as many as ten. Every family gathering and event always seems to happen at her parents' house, or at her aunt's – who lives about twenty miles away. But never here – and now she can clearly see why. The apartment is filled to the brim with books. There are books on shelves, books thrown open on the ground, books stacked on top of one another like towers, multiple books constructed to look like one giant book and even one book laying on the kitchen counter, seemingly being used as a cutting board. On it is a half-cut peach, and a knife with a sticky glow.

"Gran, do you need me to buy you a cutting board?" Dani asks.

Gran turns around with a confused gaze.

"Why would you do such a thing?" she asks.

"Well, um… I don't know really."

"OK, dear," Gran replies suspiciously. Then, she swiftly shakes her head, trying to hurl off the confusion as if it were some nagging fly. Dani swears she could see the fly, right there, circling Gran's head.

Dani slaps the fly between her hands. The smacking sound startles Gran, and she turns around to look at Dani. Immediately, another fly comes out of nowhere and begins circling, replacing its former colleague.

Perhaps Gran will have to get rid of the fly herself, Dani thinks.

"You alright dearie?" Gran asks.

"Yeah, sorry. I thought I saw a fly."

"Well, alright dear. But I don't approve of murder. no matter how insignificant your victim might seem."

Now Dani's also confused, and to make matters worse the fly is still circling Gran's head. Gran starts walking down a small hall, and soon enough, after a few seconds, the fly disappears as if into thin air. Confusion – like all feelings – is temporary.

They enter a small dark room filled with the stench of rotting paper and decked out in the glorious embellishments of neglect. There's a twin-sized bed in the back of the room – right under a dusty window – with a black bed cover printed with auburn roses and oversized thorns. Dani puts her suitcase down and goes over to the small bed. Its decorative roses are almost surrealistic considering the size of the thorns compared to that of the flower itself. It's ridiculous. It's almost hilarious, yet not quite, and yet she laughs.

"You like the bed cover?" her Gran croaks from behind her.

Dani turns her head and manages between bursts of giggles:

"Yeah, it's unusual! I like it though."

"Well, you know what they say," her gran begins, but stops. Dani waits for her to continue the rest of the sentence, yet it seems that it has already been tossed into oblivion. Gran's stare is as blank as ever.

"What do they say?" Dani tries to nudge her back.

Gran twitches her head alarmingly. She answers, "Why, they say that even the thorn's got roses."

Then, Gran simply walks out. Dani just looks at the empty doorway, her eyes beginning to eat up the entirety of her face. She bursts out in laughter.

*

After Dani settles into her room (and dusts quite a bit) she walks out only to find her Gran standing in the kitchen, cutting peaches on top of that poor old book. What does one do when one sees her own grandmother cutting up peaches on top of a book? Why, I guess one has to ask what the hell her grandmother is doing.

"Gran?"

"Yes, Bridget?"

Dani looks at Gran in shock. Had her state of mind disintegrated so badly since the last time they met? Was Gran's health more slippery than she had imagined?

Perhaps not, because suddenly Dani can see Gran's face break out into a wide smile, so large that it must be haunted by the spirit of a child. This is no health scare; this is just Gran being Gran.

"Gran, you know that's not my name."

Gran just starts laughing out maniacally. "I know!" she says, and bursts out an earthquake giggle. She begins to flail her arms around, one of which still holds the knife. She stumbles about, intoxicated by the demon child's laughter. Dani backs away after almost getting sliced open by the flailing knife in Gran's hand.

"Gran, stop! You'll hurt yourself!"

Gran laughs even harder. "You mean, I might hurt *you*?" She takes a frighteningly large leap towards Dani and points the knife sharply in her direction. Dani jumps back in horror and stumbles on a stray book, which makes her tumble down to the ground and fall straight onto her butt.

Gran is still in hysterics, but she finally puts down the knife on her makeshift cutting board. She uses her free hands to wipe away the tears rolling down her cheeks. Her laughter echoes throughout the entire apartment, and her face is glowing a bright red. Dani doesn't move. She simply remains seated on the ground, a safe distance away from the madwoman, watching the insanity unravel before her.

What have I gotten myself into…

Eventually, Gran manages to recollect herself – at least as collected as she gets.

Dani makes her way back towards the old woman, but with caution. Gran has gone back to cutting peaches atop the anonymous book.

"What did that book ever do to you?" Dani asks.

"Nothing," Gran answers, unfazed.

"Then what's the problem?"

"That's exactly the problem," Gran says. "The book did nothing for me."

Dani nods her head in understanding. She waits for Gran to continue the conversation, but Gran seems to have no intent.

"Do you want me to put on some music?" Dani asks.

"No," Gran answers simply.

"You like the silence?"

Gran looks up at her once again.

"No. But some words are as fleeting as silence. Perhaps sometimes even worse."

Dani doesn't know what to say. She has no combination of words that could touch upon the subject, so she moves on.

"Dawn is gonna come over later today and bring me some

more of my stuff."

Gran says nothing to this.

"Perhaps there is nothing to be said about facts," Dani says in her most matter-of-fact voice. She feels quite proud by this Gran-esque understanding. Yet Gran doesn't seem to agree even one bit. "It's no fact."

"But he *is* coming, Gran."

"I'll believe it when I see it," Gran says. "And even if he does come, who's to say if I'll even remember his visit after he's gone."

"Gran, even if you forget, that won't change the fact that he was here," Dani shoots back, her frustration leaking between her words.

"Oh, you're quite mistaken, my dear! Quite mistaken. Whether I remember something or not has everything to do with whether it happened."

Dani has long ago lost her patience. She decides to chop the subject off. This conversation is like a smelly patch of garlic, and right about now, all that's left is the useless scape.

"Are you making peach cobbler?"

Gran nods.

"Great, then I'll continue for you," Dani says and takes the knife out of her Gran's hand. "You go get some rest."

*

"Dzzzzzzzzzzzzz"

The buzzer of the front door screams into their little apartment.

Dani has just put the cobbler into the oven. She rubs her

hands on a stained white towel before walking to the door. There, she clicks the button on the intercom which opens the front door to the building. There's a click, the swoosh of an opening door, the hollow slaps of footsteps on stairs, and finally, *Knock knock knock* goes the door.

She opens it to see Dawn standing outside with a duffel bag hanging from each wrist. They go inside and place everything in her small bedroom. Then, they go out to sit on the only other available surface – the high chairs beside the floating minibar placed in the middle of the kitchen. They begin chatting as quietly as they can, afraid that Gran may still be in the midst of her afternoon nap.

Yet Gran surprises once again by showing up in the kitchen wearing a maroon dress that flows down to her ankles. She comes and hugs Dawn. She had seen him at quite a few family gatherings already, and that was reason enough to hug. Family, after all, are the ones who come to the overly populated, much despised Friday meals once every couple of months – aren't they?

"How are you, Ms. Porta?" Dawn asks and hugs her back heartily. Dani can see the halo floating above his head, and the devil horns growing atop his scalp.

"I'm very well, very well. You just call me Gran, alright?"

"Yes, Gran," he obeys, the same way a child obeys an adult. Dani shivers in disgust. Gran misses nothing.

"So bothered all the time! She's so bothered! Look at her," Gran says and pokes Dani in the stomach. "So bothered!"

Dawn and Gran laugh with one another and start poking Dani repeatedly. Dani is not amused by this odd joining of forces against her – she simply pushes their hands away.

"Please stop," she says, trying to reason, yet her words fly past their ears. "Dawn! Stop this shit!"

Gran stops the harassment only to say, "Don't you say words like that! I don't like that type of language."

Dani looks back at her in astonishment. Then, she turns to look at Dawn and says, "This coming from the woman who tried to *stab* me with a *kitchen knife* just an hour ago!"

Gran is giggling once again. "Oh dear! I tried to stab you, did I?" The tears are starting to pour down her cheeks once again. "Oh you poor child! So bothered!"

Dawn can't help getting seduced by the ways of blissful idiocy, and joins Gran's laughter. His laughter doesn't go unnoticed of course, not by Dani and definitely not by Gran. As Gran's laughter begins to fade, she grabs herself a cup of cold water and sips while holding the cup with both hands. She looks up and down the young man.

"You seem like an intelligent fellow," Gran says, "Let's see if you can pass my test!"

"Gran, I don't know what that entails, but I'm pretty sure that Dawn doesn't want to," Dani interjects.

"No it's alright," Dawn says. "I'll be happy to do it."

Typical.

Gran shoots Dani a victorious set of smiling eyes. She begins, "Well then, it's quite simple. I'll tell you a story and then ask you a question," Gran stops to have another sip of water. "Here goes: A tree – tall and heavy – has fallen down in the middle of a forest. No one *heard* the tree fall. No one *saw* the tree fall." Gran tilts her chin down and looks at Dawn with a face consisting solely of eyes. "If that's the case, did the tree really fall?"

Before Dawn even has a chance to open his mouth, Dani rolls her eyes wildly and simultaneously blurts out, "Gran, that's just stupid. Of course the tree fell. You just told us that it did."

"But no one heard, or saw, it fall down," Gran says matter-of-factly.

"So what? The tree fell. It's just a fact."

"Are you sure?" Gran pokes at her.

"Of course I'm sure! Gran, what's the point of this?"

"I'm just asking," Gran says. "What do you think, young man?" She turns to look at Dawn. Both sets of eyes are now bolted into his own.

"I don't know. I'm pretty sure the right answer is no – that the tree didn't fall. But I don't know why it's right…" he says.

"There is no right answer! Oh no," Gran says (and Dani rolls her eyes once again). "But personally I believe that the tree did not fall."

"Gran—"

"How come?" Dawn cuts her off. Dani bites down hard on her bottom lip.

"Well, reality is made up of our consciousness. Reality is what we see, what we feel, what we hear and touch. Reality is the world of the things that are known! And if a tree falls down without anyone's knowledge, I don't believe that it really did fall. What escapes my knowledge can never be a part of my reality. Do you understand?"

Dani can see the flies circling Dawn's head in a frenzy. She knows the answer before he speaks.

"Honestly," Dawn says, "not at all!" Both Gran and himself burst out laughing.

Dani doesn't join in. She stays mute, her bottom bolted down to the seat and her heart hanging down from the straps of her underwear. Her stare is blank, and her head is aching. She's afraid that she might have completely understood what Gran had explained. If what Gran said is true, then everyone's reality is different. What could be seen as good to one person could be seen as a tragedy to another. If what Gran said is true, then you can never quite know the people you love. You can never enter their world, not completely at least. Dani begins to feel so alone. There could be so much that she simply doesn't know. And how could she? Her reality is so limited! Her eyes can only see a certain amount, and her mind can only digest so much! How could this be true? Is it even true? It can't be. How else could she see flies and walls that aren't there?

Gran notices the vacancy of Dani's presence. She gets a feeling. She always has them, but only some are as intuitive as this. It's a feeling so strong that it's almost a belief.

"*You* did understand," Gran says, "didn't you?"

Something in Dani's eyes fills up. Suddenly they don't look so bare.

"Yeah, I think so," she says.

"What's wrong, my darling?"

"I just…" Dani tries to gather the words. "It's just that, if what you said is true, then we're all so alone. All of us are seeing the same world through separate eyes, inhaling everything differently. We can never truly know the world of the people around us. How can we even connect like that? Or love like that?"

Gran laughs, which by now is typical, almost necessary.

"I've never thought of it like that," she says. "I've always been reassured by the tree that never fell. Perhaps I'm selfish, but I always saw it as a thing playing to my advantage. Instead of thinking about some tree, I can create a whole forest inside my mind. My hands are on the wheel! No one is more in control of my life than I am, and all because my reality is my very own. I can expand it, and cut it down whenever I fancy. I can protect myself from certain 'truths' by trying to forget, and I can build whole planets that will only ever be surveyed by my own peace of mind."

"Okay," Dani says. "I agree with you about the ability to control your reality; what you believe is what you see… at least to a certain extent. But do you think that maybe some people get control from the things that they don't expect to see?"

Gran looks at her crossly. The sound of the flies around her mind is deafening.

*

The three of them share the peach cobbler Dani had finished making, while sipping from round mugs filled with scorching hot tea. Eventually, Dawn leaves after hugging Gran politely and squeezing Dani's cheeks. Then it's just the two of them. It had been a long day, and yet only the first day of their shared reality.

Dani has just finished washing the dishes when Gran suddenly calls out to her from her bedroom. Was that alarm in her voice? Dani runs as quickly as possible, fearing all that might have happened, every possibility. Perhaps Gran slipped in the shower or tripped on the corner of her bed. How in the hell had she been allowed to live all alone up until now?

At her age?!

Dani runs down the small hall and quickly reaches the front door of Gran's room. She flings it wide open, never once considering that perhaps Gran is strewn across the floor behind it. Perhaps wounded, or worse – wounded and in pain.

But alas, Gran is sitting on her bed, curled up in her lavender blanket and leaning back on a rich pile of pillows stacked up against the mahogany headboard. Gran laughs as soon as Dani's spooked expression is in view. Dani only plops onto a corner of the bed and drops her head into her hands.

"What did you want, Gran?" Dani asks through her fingers.

"I just wanted to see if you wanted to do one last thing together before I go to sleep."

"Gran, I thought something was wrong... The way you yelled for me to come? I—"

"Of course I'm alright, dearie," Gran says. "I'm just very excited that you're here. So I won't be able to fall asleep quite yet."

Dani's heart fills up with radiating waves of warmth.

"Umm, how about I read you something, Gran? I'm sure you haven't read every single book you own."

"That would be a correct assumption," Gran replies, "And even if I have read it before, I'm sure I'll enjoy it even more with you. So just pick whichever one you fancy dear. Whichever one speaks to you." She winks at Dani.

*

Dani comes back with a small book encased in patent leather coloured an olive-green. Indented into the cover, and outlined in gold, is the title:

METAMORPHOSES

"By Ovid!" Gran exclaims.

"You've read this one already?" Dani asks, displeased.

"Many times," Gran says. "It's one of my favorites."

"It looks like a collection of short stories," Dani says. "I thought that would be nice."

"Yes, all of them are great tales! They were written by a man who lived in the time of ancient Rome. His name was Ovid. Most of what we know about Greek mythology actually comes from this very book. Of course, these are only selected passages – the entire book is big enough to be a footstool!" She laughs brightly.

Dani hops onto the bed and leans on the pillows next to Gran.

"Which one do you want to read tonight, Gran?"

"Oh, no no no. We can't simply start reading. First I need to teach you the basic principles of mythology," Gran says.

Oh no no no no no no no, Dani thinks.

*

But alas – yes.

Gran says that you can't read Greek mythology without having the key to understand; and lucky for them, Gran has the key. So Dani listens.

Gran says that on one hand there are the gods. On the other – the cosmic reality. This reality has laws and forces which the gods themselves have to abide by, for example; the gods must drink and sleep, and although they are gods, they are prone to get hurt.

Even so, the cosmic reality isn't always the reigning queen – sometimes the gods are the imperative. Gran says that they 'keep you guessing'.

Gran speaks of witches, queer women assassins, men made of marble and snakes as big as houses. Dani is partly entranced, and utterly confused. However, it's not the type of confusion that births ache between the folds of your forehead, it's the type that allows you to bask inside it in peace. Dani feels safe inside the turmoil of her mind, and eventually, a clear thought rises from the soot. It speaks:

I think I'm going to like this book.

It's a simple thought, almost childlike in its manner and simplicity, and yet it spreads a smile on her lips. Lips of a grown woman stepping out into the world. Not the world of today, but the one thousands of years before herself, and it makes her feel brand-new.

Eventually, Gran says that she's ready to go to bed. Dani asks if perhaps she should start reading, but Gran says that she's too tired. She wants to sleep.

Dani walks out of the room and turns off the light. A slippery little ball drops down to the pit of her stomach and melts into sour disappointment. It's a papercut version of devastation, but we all know that those motherfuckers sting like hell.

5. Luca

Most days, she feels like a balloon. Hollow, floating through life, grazing only her toes on the ground as she passes through this world, never fully experiencing what it's truly like to live. She doesn't fly and she never walks. She's like those sad helium balloons that mope around your house after only a few days of being airborne. She keeps expecting to drop to the floor, but life offers no such release.

The only thing she drops onto is her creamy bed. It's the only way to knock the wind out of her. She's a peculiar type of balloon, a balloon which only round corners and fluff threaten to pop its alien skin.

She can stay strong when you cut and burn her. She stays strong when she cuts and burns herself. Yet when she falls onto her bed after a long day (or anytime really) she can feel her head pop, she can hear her bones spewing out their mass. In seconds, she is but a thin slice of deflated plastic strewn across her butterfly blanket. She lays in her toxic fumes and gags on them. She despises her thin lungs – lungs made for choking, lungs made for dying.

She wants to die. She knows how to die. She picks up a

bottle of Advil and spills the content of its guts onto her blanket. She does the same thing with her brand-new cardboard boxes filled with encased pills. She swallows them, three each time until they're all gone. Not gone… but put to good use. She knows how to die – I told you so.

Yet she does none of this. Something keeps holding her alive. It might be the antidepressants she started taking around a month ago. Those things – those round, sickly mint green pills with a gash in the centre – have been affecting her. So far, they've done nothing for her mental state, and everything for her physical. Her hunger has dissipated almost completely. She has headaches so sharp they could cut through steel. Not only are her headaches lethal, they're also incredibly diverse in their nature; they're not always sharp, for sometimes they're dull, aching everywhere and nowhere at once, trapping in radiations of pain like a bomb waiting to go off.

There's also the nightmares, the graphic, illustrative nightmares that seem so real even ten minutes after waking up. After these nightmares, she always wakes up rattled, her pyjamas drenched, her body lying in a puddle of her sweat. The first time it happened, she was positive that the sheath of ocean around her had popped, yet upon further inspection of her enveloped body she finds no holes, cracks, or tears… who knows how this thing around her should even come apart.

Everything is shit. The world is idle, with no room for true rapture. She definitely doesn't feel pleasure of any sort, and if she does, it's not quite the real thing, not the pleasure she once used to feel (did she ever, though? If she ever did feel it at all – she suddenly can't remember). Luca's experience of pleasure these days is like dipping french fries inside a tomato;

it's doubtlessly not ketchup, definitely not the real thing, yet it's not so far off that its nature is unidentifiable.

TV gives her a certain type of pleasure. A submerging pleasure rooted in anguish. She watches TV shows, and movies on her laptop, while cocooned inside her butterfly blanket. She usually watches TV shows, especially meaningless reality TV, because movies feel like too much of a commitment (even though her only engagement is the screen). The only movies she manages to convince herself to watch are horror films. And the best types of horror films are the ones that she's already seen. It's much easier to commit to something you already have in your head.

She loves horror films because they calm her. For an hour and a half, and sometimes two, she's afraid of the monster under her bed, or the killer in her closet. She's afraid of unreality instead of sinking into the truth.

She watches her silly shows, sometimes with her head turned away from the screen. She keeps watching as faint hunger creeps in, thirst screams to be quenched and urine builds up inside her. She always waits until the last possible second to get up and use the bathroom.

She's forever curled up into herself, trapped inside a body she feels so utterly removed from. At least once a day, her sister brings food up to her bed after she gets back from work (where does she work again? It doesn't matter. Nothing does.) Luca always thanks her in a whisper, but only because it's required. Only because it comes out naturally enough.

She would say that her soul is someplace else, but these days she doubts if she's even got one.

*

It's that time of the week again – her meeting with Ms. Porcelain. She needs to get out of her bed. She needs to put on clothes, real clothes; never jeans, they're too uncomfortable. Always the same pair of sweats, and an oversized T with a long-sleeved shirt underneath to cover up her arms. Then it's out to daylight, which burns like acid pouring into her eyes. Eyes that have been scorched from the infinite, faint glow of her laptop screen.

She walks over to her bike, still in their usual place – never misbehaving, and yet… disappointing. Disappointing. Today, for the first time.

Disappointing? Strangely so.

Somehow their usual aura is invisible to her eyes. Perhaps even comfort and routine have stopped ploughing their way through her mind. Or maybe it's her – it probably is. Maybe she's all fucked up; too rocky to even plough.

She looks down at her body, completely encompassed by water. She looks at her hands, wrinkly and pale, surrounded by mittens of liquid. Suddenly, her whole body starts to burn, especially her eyes, so she quickly closes them shut. She feels as though her entire body is an open wound, and some unmerciful being is pouring salt all over. She shrieks at the top of her lungs, her eyes still closed. The burning sensation takes its time to dwell, feeding on her ache and misery – as all bad times do.

After a few minutes Luca becomes accustomed to her new burden, and with this surrender comes the suppression of pain. She uses it to open her eyes. Everything seems to be the same. Water still surrounds her from head to toe. Everything is just the same as it wa——

Oh dear lord. Oh my god. Oh my god, what was that? Luca finally feels panic's claws slicing their way into her heart. *It can't be. I'm imagining this.*

Yet it happens again. A colourful fish swerves its way in front of Luca's vision. There it goes again. Again. And again. Luca identifies it as a parrotfish, which unsurprisingly is well-known to be a saltwater fish.

Luca dares to look down towards her stomach and legs. An entire school of miniature parrotfish swims around the ocean that surrounds her. Every fish looks exactly the same as the others; a turquoise body with bubblegum pink spots, an orange belly, neon yellow side fins and purple rouge spread on both cheeks as if it were applied by a child.

Luca's eyes are stapled to her thighs, watching the fish swim around them in circles, never knowing when to stop, never being able to. Her second skin is packed to the brim with these Mediterranean fish. She sits down on the sidewalk, just in case she suddenly faints. Yet she only feels worse.

She lays her back on the concrete without thinking twice. She can feel the blood gushing back up to her head, providing a constant, tickling rush to her temples.

She decides to ditch her bike that morning and takes the bus instead.

*

Luca sits in the back of the bus on one of its worn-out, obnoxiously blue, cushioned seats. She struggles to squeeze on her headphones. They used to fit perfectly, that is before she had an astronaut helmet filled with fish around her head.

When she finally manages to snap the headphones around her thoughts, she settles on a random song and turns the volume all the way up. Usually, full volume makes her brain thump, and her eardrums burst. However now, through the ocean around her, the music sounds muffled and far away, barely caressing her ears. She thumps her head almost violently onto the glass window beside her and watches the world pass by. Her head would probably hurt from the hit of the glass if it wasn't for the liquid around her softening the blow, making the pain nonexistent. Either way, nothing could be worse than the pain inside her.

Uselessly, helplessly, Luca presses on the button that turns up the volume, which allows her to keep pressing even when she's at full volume. What a merciless button.

Luca decides to focus on all the happenings outside of the window. The world is still asleep under the cover of the winter skies, yet there seem to be some people who didn't cave and crumble from the numbness around them. She sees blurry children with school uniforms running into a candy kiosk, a young woman passing on a yellow bike, and an old couple sitting on a bench with squinting eyes, withering away like two raisins in the gloomy light.

As Luca is leaning her head on the window, losing herself in the world outside of the moving metal box, a young man sitting a few rows in front of her turns his head around in curiosity. His eyes automatically fish her out in between the rows of ocean chairs. His eyes linger on her. This young man has a world of his own, completely unrelated to Luca's, and their worlds will never overlap again. However, at this moment he's looking at our Luca and admiring her beauty.

Yes, she's beautiful. He might've found her beautiful even if he knew that she was drowning, or better yet, even if he saw the ocean that surrounds her. He doesn't, though. He only sees a beautiful girl with an absent stare. He lifts his eyes to look at the top of her head, where her golden curls coil around the cream-coloured strap of her headphones. He slowly pans down to her lips, shut tight like a trap. He goes all the way down to her shoulders covered with a basic black t-shirt, and that's where the rest of her body disappears behind the seat in front of her. He turns his head back to look out of his window, and never thinks of her again.

*

Fifteen minutes later Luca arrives at the front entrance of Juvo 16. She goes up the stairs and into the apartment with the number 2 proudly hung on its door. She knocks. After Ms. Porcelain opens the door for her, and they're both sitting down on the identical beige comforters placed directly in front of each other, they begin to talk. They talk for a while, not really saying much, until Ms. Porcelain says, "What do you feel that you get out of our meetings?"

Luca's skin shivers from the staggering propriety of the question. She tries to find words, but they've all run away to a desolate corner deep within her stomach. The condensed lump of frightened words explodes, causing a sharp pain to shoot through her lower abdomen. Helplessly, Luca tries to piece together different combinations of the 26 letters of the English language until she comes up with an ever so classy, "Umph…"

"It's okay," Ms. Porcelain interjects her pathetic attempt. "I just want you to know that I really do want to help you. I really think that I *can* help you. What do *you* think?"

Luca's tongue finally attracts the right words and releases them. "I don't know." Not a very efficient bunch of words, but they help bring on the end of the beginning.

"I can't help you if you don't believe that I can," Ms. Porcelain says.

Luca suddenly realises that Ms. Porcelain is quite beautiful, despite her slicked back, stuck-up appearance.

"I don't know," Luca answers simply, slightly ashamed for genuinely not knowing.

"You know, you've spoken a bit about your previous therapists. Based on your stories, my biased generalised assumption is that they've all been psychologists. I hope you know, or at least remember, that I'm not."

This snatches Luca's attention. Curiosity rushes through her veins, and the water around her loses the majority of its burdening nature.

"I'm a psychoanalyst. I do things, or at least I hope I do things, differently than psychologists. I allow myself to say more. And dare I say that to me, looking from the outside, it seems like you're drowning."

Luca feels her heart drop down to her bladder. She looks down at her thighs and sees that the liquid which surrounds her has started seeping out of an unseen hole. Slowly, liquid keeps spilling out of her ocean and onto the floor. The water starts to pile up in the small therapy room.

In seconds, the water is up to her knees, and the pace of its growth only fastens. When the water level comes up to her stomach, Luca watches as the first parrotfish finds its way out of her capsule and out to the room that surrounds her. Slowly, everything is flowing out of her, and the water level keeps rising higher and higher, filling up with more and more parrotfish. The colourful pool keeps rising higher until it reaches Luca's chin. Luca Looks over at Ms. Porcelain and sees that the water has managed to reach up to her shoulders. Both of them are sitting inside Luca's ocean, now and then feeling the scaly skin of the fish caress their outer arm or leg. The room is small and floating with life.

Luca dips the back of her head into the water and runs a dripping arm through her damp curls. Finally, she can feel her scalp instead of the jello-like exterior of the capsule that surrounded her ocean. Finally, the ocean is released. Finally, it has transformed.

Ms. Porcelain respectfully keeps her silence, allowing Luca to stay uninterruptedly idle in the reality that they share, while her true presence grazes on places beyond Ms. Porcelain's sight.

6. Dani

Dani is walking through the streets of Telo. She has Gran's grocery list written and memorised in the back of her mind; another block or two and she'll be at the closest kiosk. She walks slowly, unbothered, while listening to the latest Nirvana album, which honestly she doesn't entirely get. The streets are familiar, mostly because they're all more of the same. It's not an unfortunate repetitiveness – Telo is beautiful in its own dishevelled, friendly way.

Eventually Dani makes it to the kiosk. She begins to pile groceries inside the plastic shopping basket while walking through the aisles filled with colourful plastic and logoed brand names. She passes the canned goods, runs her hand atop the watermelons in the fruit and vegetable aisle and lastly grabs a Snickers bar from the candy section.

The items on the list are all checked off, including a few improvisations. Dani makes her way to the register. Behind the counter is a young girl, seemingly around Dani's age. She has long, lime-green hair mixed with some streaks of chartreuse. She has wispy bangs that fall down to her light, barely visible brows, which stand no chance of recognition being right above the largest pair of green eyes that Dani had ever seen. The girl looks like a cross between a swamp witch and a supermodel.

"Miss?"

The word finally reaches Dani's ears.

"Yes, yes, hi," she says and starts taking the groceries out of the basket and onto the counter. The girl with the green hair smiles kindly and starts scanning the groceries. Dani doesn't dare to look up at her again.

Suddenly a voice rises from somewhere within the maze of aisles, asking for assistance. The girl with the green hair speaks into the intercom, asking for an employee to 'assist the person in aisle 4'. Then, she continues to scan and bag Dani's groceries.

Not a minute passes before that same voice speaks out loud and clear, claiming to have gotten no assistance. The girl with the green hair tells Dani to wait while she steps out to help. Dani nods without looking up.

Three minutes go by. Then another two, and the girl still hasn't come back. Dani looks around to see if she can spot her, but while she's looking about, the girl steps out of a midsection aisle, seemingly headed right back to the register. Dani means to pull her eyes away from the girl, but her glare is strung taut. At first, she can't explain why she's simply unable to look away, but the following seconds buy her a clue – a clue which all of a sudden morphs into a big white snowball of understanding that slams right into her head.

The girl with the green hair is *floating*. She's hovering just a few inches above the ground, seemingly walking on air. Her large burgundy skirt is fluttering in the still and unidentifiable breeze of the kiosk as she float-walks her way back to the counter.

Dani's face must have revealed the state of her mind, because instead of apologising for the wait, the first thing the girl with the green hair says is, "Are you alright?"

Dani looks behind her; she sees people wandering around the kiosk unbothered, as if no one had just floated over the path that they now walk. It's impossible; more so the fact that no one else saw it rather than the whole floating business. It just can't be.

Dani had gotten used to seeing flies, and pearls, and even walls slowly claiming their presence, but a person floating? For some reason, that seems to be in a league of its own.

Even so, the world must keep spinning, in the same way that words must come out of her mouth. "Yeah, sorry, I'm fine," Dani says. Empty words sent out to reclaim her sanity, or at the very least dress up her insanity.

Dani quickly walks out of the shop, one plastic bag in each hand. She walks fiercely through the streets, making her way back mindlessly through the path that she had gone before.

*

Later on that same day, Gran and herself are walking through the streets with no particular plan or direction. Gran has her arm wrapped around Dani's, and she leans on her ever so slightly as they walk. Dani has found these walks to be two things: 1. Nice, because it gives her a sense of being needed, and 2. Absolutely, intolerably pointless. She is yet to realise in what way Gran benefits from these walks. Sure, some days it's the only time she steps out of the house, but most days Gran has a million other things; drawing classes, her bridge club, cafe with friends… and yet every single day – with no exceptions – Gran and herself take a walk. What is it with old people and walks?

Dani hasn't been with Gran long enough for it to become a tradition, so currently, she regards these daily walks as a 'moronic habit'. They walk away from home and eventually make their way back towards it. The walk back is seemingly silent, but Dani's mind is violent. She doesn't exactly have thoughts – everything inside her mind is flashing by too quickly, with barely enough time to recognise its actuality.

Gran doesn't say anything either, yet her mind doesn't seem blank; with a simple glance Dani can see that. Gran has multiple glowing rings of light circling her head, bringing to mind outer space, and extraterrestrial planets. Her mind is in a different place, a different world.

*

When they get home, Gran sits down on the little burgundy couch floating above a sea of scattered books. Dani sits down next to her, feeling almost obliged to do so.

"Gran, do you remember when we talked about the tree that didn't fall?"

"How could I forget?"

"Well…" She hesitates. "What if no one but myself can see it fall?"

"If you were around to watch the tree fall, then I suppose it did exactly that – at least in your reality…. And the reality of others who choose to believe you full-heartedly, of course.”

“No, that’s not what I mean,” Dani thinks of how to phrase what’s in her mind. ”What if I didn’t exactly *experience* the tree falling, but I still know that it fell. Not because someone told me, but because I somehow *know* it. Like having a dream. Like a prophecy almost… a prophecy that already played out… I don’t know what I’m saying.”

Gran doesn’t answer.

“I…” Dani doesn’t know how else to put it. “What if someone told me that the tree fell, and I can see, like *really* see in their face that they’re telling the truth.”

“What would you see in that case?” Gran asks.

“I mean, I’m not sure. But maybe if they were lying I would see their nose begin to grow like Pinocchio. Or maybe if they were lying I would see their tongue split in half at the tip… like, you know, the tongue of a snake.”

“And when you say see, you mean—”

“*Really see.*”

Gran doesn’t say anything for a while. The silence is devastatingly still.

When Gran finally does speak, the words are completely untethered from the situation. “I’m going to take a shower, dear. Maybe later you’ll come to my room and we’ll start reading that book of ours.”

“Metamorphoses,” Dani says silently, her answer a lending hand towards the conversation’s demise.

Gran nods and gets up. She turns to Dani, puts her hand under her chin, and stares into her eyes for a minute. Dani can’t see anything in her face – maybe she still needs time to think. Finally, Gran flashes her a crooked smile and turns to leave.

*

They're both sitting on Gran's bed, Gran under the blanket and Dani over it.

"Which one do you want to read first, Gran?"

"Let's read the one about Echo and Narcissus," Gran answers in a flash.

Dani flips through the book until she finds the story. She begins, "When Narcissus was born, the blind prophet Tiresias told his mother that he was to live as long as he did not truly know himself."

What's the problem? Dani thinks to herself, *Break all the mirrors in the house. How are you supposed to know yourself if you can't even see yourself?*

Dani is about to continue when a rebutting thought strikes:

Wait, then what about the blind... do they not know their true selves? Maybe you can turn a blind eye towards some part of yourself and still know your true self... right? I mean, after all, what you believe is true is by all means your truth... and there isn't any higher truth, is there? I guess it's all explained in the tree that didn't fall. What you don't know, or don't believe, can't ever be a part of your reality. Even so, I think I'm still missing something here. There's another element to this story that I haven't been introduced to.

"Narcissus was beautiful. All the girls were after him, and so were all the boys, yet Narcissus showed no interest in any of them. One day, while he was wandering in the woods, a nymph named Echo noticed him. Echo instantly fell in love with Narcissus, yet she could not call to him, for she could only repeat words that were said to her.

"Eventually, Narcissus heard a rustle somewhere in the

bushes, and called out, 'Who is it?' and Echo replied with those same words. Other words echoed back and forth between the two souls until Narcissus managed to track down her location. Now they were face to face.

"Being so close made Narcissus freak. He pushed away her love and admiration, the same way he had always rejected such feelings from others. He never let anyone get too close.

"Echo was heartbroken, and crushed into the sharpest pieces of devastation.

"One day, one of Narcissus' many rejected admirers cried out to the gods, praying that one day Narcissus would fall helplessly in love with someone he could not have.

"From the words of a desperate woman sent to the gods, a prophecy was born. And like every prophecy worth telling – this one also played out.

"Eventually the day came when Narcissus stumbled upon a silvery lake in the middle of the woods. Around the clear waters of the lake lay a cushion of grass bathing in gentle rays of sunlight. Narcissus gave way to his temptation to approach the scene—"

"Why shouldn't he, right?" Gran says and nudges Dani with her elbow.

"What? Gran, please, I'm trying to read."

Gran slips out a slippery giggle. She glides her locked thumb and forefinger over her pressed lips and gestures throwing away the key. Dani looks at her in disbelief for a few moments longer. Only when the silence ensues, and Gran's lips remain shut, Dani – content now – continues. "Narcissus saw his reflection in that mirror lake. He immediately fell in love with the image before his eyes. The image of himself."

Hey! I guess I was kind of on the nose with the whole mirror idea! Except, here he doesn't know that he's looking at himself... he thinks it's 'another'.

"Narcissus could not understand why the boy disappeared every time he tried to reach out his hand to him. Every time he touched the surface of the lake, reaching for the boy trapped underwater, his image would disappear.

"Narcissus could see that when he spoke, the boy in the lake was trying to speak back, and when he cried, so did the boy. If they both felt the same way, why couldn't they be united?

"Eventually, Narcissus understood that the image in the lake was none other than his own. He was the one lighting the fire, *and* the one burning within its flames.

"Can I highlight in your book?" Dani asks.

Gran's wrinkles vanish as her skin is strung taut by a smile.

Dani runs out to get a highlighter, and when she gets back, she highlights that last sentence with a yellow glow. Then, the end ensues. "Narcissus crumbled from ache. Both him and his reflection disappeared. All that was left of him was a pale daffodil, with its golden crown, growing right at the edge of the water."

Dani says no more.

"It's the end, isn't it," Gran nods lightly. "You know, in other, better languages than our own, the daffodil is called a Narciss."

Dani doesn't hear this, for her mind is heavily echoing from the drop of a sudden realisation.

"Is this where the word narcissism comes from?"

Gosh, I'm a modern-day genius, I am. A real-life prodigy of the mind.

However, Gran's starless eyes seem to say otherwise. She answers, "Yes, I suppose so."

Dani can feel her face burn from the inside out.

"The real question is," Gran says, "is how did falling in love fulfil the prophecy from the beginning of the story? The one that said that he shall live as long as he doesn't know himself."

Dani doesn't know what to say.

"Think about it. I'm going to bed now dearie; good night." Gran kisses Dani on the forehead, and Dani feels like a little girl again. A stupid little girl. So small, so small.

*

Dani walks out of Gran's room, feeling the smallest she's ever felt. She thinks about Alice in Wonderland, when she drank from a potion standing on a glass table. Upon drinking it, Alice shrunk down to a size so small she could no longer reach the top of the table – where coincidentally, she had left a very important key. That particular key would've allowed her to open a small door, for reasons unknown to anyone besides herself; she simply *needed* to pass through.

Dani felt as Alice did on that day. She knew the answer to Gran's question, but only when it was too late. Now Gran was asleep and she couldn't – or at least shouldn't – wake her up just to give her a damn key. It doesn't matter that she can see the key standing high up on the glass table. The table is still standing between them, now farther away than ever.

It doesn't matter that she knows exactly why falling in love made Narcissus truly know himself. It doesn't matter that only through loving another you're able to know your true self. After all, how would you know what you are if you have no one to compare yourself to? Yet for others to exist, you must acknowledge their existence. And what's a better way to acknowledge the existence of others than by loving them (or hating them perhaps)? How would you know what it is to love if you have no one to fall in love with? What can fill your heart except others?

7. Luca

When Luca steps out of her meeting with Ms. Porcelain, she learns a significant truth. Her ocean had, no doubt, gone through a metamorphosis. However, it was far more substantial than she had imagined. Her ocean had, of course, spilled out into the little room where she and Ms. Porcelain had their meeting. However, it had also somehow infected the entire world with its entity.

When Luca steps out of Ms. Porcelain's clinic, she sees that the entire stairway is filled to the brim with ocean water. Parrotfish are swerving and dancing all around the railways, and some are rubbing their bellies on the stairs. The water is so clear, it could easily be mistaken for air, yet Luca knows better. Luca starts making her way down the steps, fighting hard to keep her feet on the ground. Her body keeps wanting to rise up into the ocean around her.

Eventually, she gives in to the buoyancy and starts breaststroking her way downstairs. She swims over the railing and starts plummeting down into the empty space in the middle of the spiralling stairs. She pushes dense chunks of liquid away from her face as she dives vertically down towards the ground floor of the apartment building. Luca closes her eyes, puts her arms to her sides, and listens as her body slowly drops, cutting right through the ocean all around her, like a toothpick pushed into a block of butter.

When she opens her eyes again, she sees a ray of light seeping in through the front entrance of the building. She slips into the light and swims towards the door. She pushes the glass door open and floats her way into the street.

The streets are empty as she's hovering above the concrete, swerving her way towards the nearest bus stop. Luca spins the front of her body towards the sky and starts to backstroke lazily. There's no visible end to the ocean up above; even the clouds are nowhere near the unseen surface of the water. There's no sun in the sky, yet her rays are seeping in through the dense gallons of water and falling onto Luca's face; caressing her cheeks, tingling her eyelashes and lovingly toasting her nose.

Soon enough – after a euphoria that cannot be measured by time – Luca arrives at the bus station. She flips around in the water, feeling herself dangle on the verge of a giggle. She's almost content, almost at peace with her own private world.

Just as she's dangling from the cliff of ease and looking into its blissful abyss, Luca sees another girl standing at the bus station beside her. Instantly, she feels her body being involuntarily pushed down. Before she has a moment to allow wonderment to take its place, her feet are stapled to the ground and she's standing upright with her arms beside her body.

Luca looks over at the girl standing a few feet away from her, swiping through her phone.

What the hell did you just do? A long, accusing finger in her mind points sharply towards the anonymous girl.

It doesn't matter. Nothing good ever lasts in my world.

*

A few minutes later Luca is on the bus, on her way back home. She's sitting in the back once again, her body glued to the seat. She tries to lift herself up through the water, but with no such luck. Now the ocean only seems to be weighing her down. On the contrary, since regaining her sense of gravity, her ocean has become a million times more fruitful.

For instance, she can see a young sea turtle floating over the front two seats on the right side of the bus. There's a large spotted manta ray repeatedly circling just below the metal roof. Outside of Luca's window, she watches as they pass by a grand blue whale, hovering slightly above the sidewalk, stretching out for three whole blocks. The entire city is brimming with life. The overruling majority is parrotfish – now ten times the size they were when trapped inside Luca's shell. Now that her ocean has stopped weighing down her heart, and infected her mind, its power is immense – its presence is everywhere.

Even when she gets back home and sits down on the butterfly blanket on top of her bed, she sees a large sunfish floating around in front of her window, its body seemingly vacuumed onto the glass. She gets up and opens her window slowly. At first, the sunfish alarmingly removes himself from the glass and stays outside of her bedroom. However, on second thought, he starts to clumsily creep inside.

He eventually settles lazily under Luca's desk, and she can almost hear him sigh.

"I get it, Fred," Luca says. Then, on second thought she says, "You don't mind if I call you Fred, do you?"

Fred blows out two alarmingly deformed bubbles.

*

Luca can't fall asleep that night. She gets out of bed, and before she even realises what she's doing she's on the seat of her bike, speeding through the impenetrable darkness of the night. She didn't think she would ever ride her bike again, and yet emptiness eventually found superiority over exhaustion.

*

Once again Luca is flying through the streets of Telo on her bike. It's four in the morning, and the city has finally gone to sleep. Every bar is closed, and every apartment is pitch-black. There's no one alive in the world but herself. Her brain is blasting with songs coming through her headphones. Usually Luca likes to listen to the lyrics, but not now; now she can only hear the bass, the kick and the gibberish words floating in harmony.

Luca's feet melt into the pedals as she spins them faster and faster until she can hear the woosh of air splitting around her body. She can hear the air scream even through the blasting music.

The music from her headphones now seems to be coming from everywhere; falling from the trees, singing from the sky, leading her forward and pushing her from behind. No matter where she looks, there's music, and the only thing she feels is free. She screams along to the lyrics she knows, not thinking in sentences, yet meaning each word. She screams at the top of her lungs, and nobody wakes up – and for the first time, she's glad that they're asleep.

Luca spots a steep avenue up ahead, and without thinking about where it leads, she turns towards it. She starts her decline, but it's still not fast enough, so she spins the pedals until her thighs go numb. Luca closes her eyes and takes a deep breath into her lungs, soaking up every bit of air she can get. She has never felt so full, so content, so incredibly... excited. The type of excitement that crawls from your lower abdomen and straight into your throat. The type that gives you chills in the back of your head and a heartbeat in the tips of your fingers.

Luca keeps her eyes shut. She soaks up the moment, feeling double everything now that she's blind. Luca's bike keeps shooting down the avenue. Her eyes are still closed when her bike slams into a streetlamp. Luca's eyes are still closed when she flies off her bike and slams down onto the pavement. Her skin rips all over as her body tumbles to a stop.

Finally, Luca opens her eyes. Almost everything is gone. The music, the ecstasy, her Beats headphones. The only thing left now is the ocean all around her; teasing her with its existence, screaming at her, 'You can lose everything, and you'll still have me'.

*

Luca gets back home at dawn. She hobbles up the stairs, into the apartment, and straight towards the bathroom. She begins to fill up their small tub with warm water. She laughs (out loud!) at the sight of seeing a bathtub getting filled up when she knows full well that the entire world around her is already submerged in water. Courage comes along with her laughter, so she slips her naked body into the steaming tub.

Everything burns. All the cuts and scrapes from the fall. It burns bad, but not for too long. Soon enough she's relishing in the slickness of the tub, and the warm water no longer burns, but simply hugs. Her cheeks are flushed with heat, her eyes are closed and her worries are far, far away. Her hair is a jungle of chocolate-covered vines strewn upon the slick outskirts of the bath.

Rosy light seeps in through the bathroom window and floods the room with rouge. The only sound is a gentle 'splish splash' as Luca raises her hands out of the water and tenderly glazes her face with a fresh coat of liquid. The bloody cuts and scrapes are tenderising in the humidity and moisture, while stinging divinely. Every part of her body is tingling with sensibility, and her brain is finally slumbered.

She's sitting in her grime, and she can see it with her eyes – floating clots of blood and dirt in the now-tepid water of the bath. It's so nice to see instead of feel. It's kind on the heart, and ever so easy for the brain to process.

It's so nice to see instead of feel.

It's so nice to see instead of feel.

Suddenly, Luca knows what to do. She can see even more than she sees now, she can feel even less than she already does. She suddenly realises how she can make this moment last, how she can make sure that it never goes away.

She reaches for the razor laying on the shelf beside the tub.

It's so nice to see instead of feel.

It's so nice to see instead of feel.

The bathtub turns into a dusty pink mist that slowly spreads and turns into a rich cranberry red. In minutes, Luca is sitting in a thick burgundy soup of her insides.

She's lightheaded, and her hands are tingling as if millions of tiny fairies are dancing around on her skin. The world is cloudy, falling apart. She looks down at the tub, and swirls her hand around the dense fluid, barely feeling its touch upon her skin.

Suddenly she does feel something. A strange jellylike lump floating inside the water. She moves her hand away from it in disgust, only to bump into another gooey clump. No matter where she moves there's another, and another, and another. She can feel the lumps all around her now, gently pressing on her naked skin.

"What the hell is this??" She can swear that she had screamed this out loud, but alas, it was just a thought.

Then the first lump pops up on the surface of the water. It's covered in blood, so it's hard to make out exactly what it is. Another one pops up right next to where her knee is peaking out of the water. Another one next to her right shoulder, another over her stomach, another two next to her right foot, four on her left, another, and another, and another... and soon the blood slowly slips off the lumps and their true skin is uncovered.

It's parrotfish. Hundreds of them floating on the surface of the burgundy water. Just floating, not moving or flapping about, but simply floating with their mouths open. They're dead. They're all dead. They're all dead and she too will be dead soon.

Regret begins to wrap around her like fog. As it thickens, it starts to press on the rooms of her heart. The regret is there, but it's not quite enough to supply movement to her quickly numbing limbs. Our Luca is slowly but surely fading away, and escaping out of this world.

As she keeps bleeding out, the regret finally manages to puncture her heart. Immediately, her chest springs up in a bolt, and a thick gasp escapes the grasp of her teeth. The entire room shakes to the sound of her voice.

She can hear her heart thump inside her throat. She's back. At least for now. Without thinking too much, she raises a shaky arm towards her towel. She reaches as far as she can, and when that isn't enough, she reaches even further, until her fingers come in touch with the towel. In a swift motion, she grabs it and quickly presses it onto her wrist. She presses long and hard. She presses so the blood will stop flowing. She presses for her life.

Time goes by without identification. Luca's head is leaned back on the skirt of the tub, her eyes are closed and she's still pressing the towel on her wrist. Without opening her eyes, she feels around the tub for the knob that drains out the water. Her hand comes in touch with it, and the frostiness of the metal slices her skin, and she can't help but shriek through her teeth. Despite the pain, she twists the knob and listens as the drain pops and the burgundy water starts flowing down into oblivion – thank god.

When she hears the last of the water pass through the drain, she opens her eyes to see the white bathtub dappled with maroon clumps, all the surviving blood clots still hanging onto the surface of the tub. She feels a stingy acid rise in her throat, so she quickly moves the towel to her mouth. But now there's blood all over her face. She should've known; the towel was soaked through with it. Her cheeks fill up with vomit as she removes the sticky towel from her lips. She can feel the tears rise in her eyes, but she fights them off and forces herself to swallow the vomit. She gulps it down.

Without looking at her injured wrist, she throws out the bloody towel, stands up in the tub and reaches for the shower head, resting on its holder above her head. She uses it to wash off all the clumps that adorn the curved, glassy skin of the tub. When she's all done, she washes the blood off of herself and gets out of the shower, still not managing to get herself to look at the wound on her wrist.

Luca wraps herself up with her sister's towel and looks around the bathroom. Everything is as it was. As if nothing had happened.

But something did happen, it did.

Luca bends down and picks up the bloody towel. She holds it in her hands for a while, looking around helplessly. An idea strikes her: she opens up a cabinet under the sink, exposing all of the plumbing pipes. She stuffs the bloody towel inside and closes it shut. Then she takes a snowball of toilet paper, wets it with some water and cleans the specks of blood left over on the floor from where the towel had been. She looks around the room for any further evidence, but finds none.

And that's how you get away with murder, ladies and gentleman.

With her sister's towel wrapped around her, she slowly opens the bathroom door, trying to cause the least amount of sound possible. She sticks out her head and sees that the space is clear. The hall in front of her is coloured a musky pink, telling her that it's still early. She sneaks out of the door and tiptoes at rapid speed towards her room. The second she gets inside she shuts the door behind her, turns the lock and drops her body down onto the bed.

She almost falls asleep from exhaustion, but quickly realises that she's still not in the clear. She gets up and finds an old, thin, white shirt in her closet that she barely wears anymore. She cuts out a long rectangle of fabric from it with a pair of scissors and wraps it around the wound on her wrist, still without looking at the damage. She ties the end of the fabric with a safety pin she finds strewn on the corner of her desk. Then, she quickly gets dressed into a thick, oversized top, and the first pair of pants she gets a hold of. She grabs the towel on her bed, planning to return it to the bathroom, but, at the last second, she notices a bloody stain imprinted on the side of it. She fucked up.

It's okay, she'll fix it.

Come on, keep going, she says to herself. *Just a little more.*

She takes the towel, goes back into the bathroom, takes the second towel from under the sink and quickly rushes towards the kitchen. When she gets there, she bullets straight to the kitchen sink. Under the kitchen sink she opens a cabinet and takes out a trash bag and drops both of the towels inside. Quickly, she hurries out of the apartment door, down the stairs and out into the street. She locks her eyes with the nearest trash bin and throws the evidence into its empty belly.

Then, she's back up in the house, taking two fresh towels out of her closet and placing them on their hangers in the bathroom. She takes a wet wipe and cleans the bloody pipes under the sink.

You did it. It's done.

*

Luca sleeps for the rest of that day.

8. Dani

"Ouch!"

Dani had just been cutting a fruit salad on top of another let-down book.

"What happened, dear?" Gran lifts her eyes from her embroidery to look at Dani.

"I'm fine, I just cut my finger on this knife. Can you get me a band-aid?"

Gran gives her a band-aid and a kiss. The knife had taken one hell of a slice out of her finger. She rinses the cut under cold water and uses a paper towel to dry it, stopping the bleeding for just enough time to wrap the band-aid around it. Dani leaves the book, the knife and the bloody apple. She sits down in a bar chair next to Gran.

Gran is embroidering embellishments in the centre of a small cotton patch; a pattern that seems to be making some sort of flower. Dani soon realises that it's the beginning of a daffodil — a Narciss.

Gran notices Dani's wondering eyes.

"I've decided to make a patch for each metamorphosis that we read! Eventually, I'll be able to make you a blanket out of it! How nice would that be?"

"Very nice, Gran," Dani says.

Well, it's no dream of mine, but it's a sweet gesture.

"Want me to read you some more while you work?"

"Sure, dear. I have about an hour before I go out to have lunch with your mother."

"You're going out for lunch? Then why am I making us a fruit salad, Gran?"

"I don't know, dear," Gran says through a giggle. "But you look cute as a peach making it."

Dani rolls her eyes. Gran notices, of course.

"I don't understand how you don't have a constant headache from all those eye-rolls you give out so generously," Gran says.

Dani rolls her eyes again, and Gran doesn't miss a moment of it. She begins to bellow out crackling laughter – the kind of laughter you would expect to hear from a cartoon witch.

Dani gives Gran a disapproving look, and just as she turns her eyes away from her, shock pulls her glance right back.

Gran's face is different. What is it?

It's like looking at someone without their glasses on for the first time. Like seeing Santa after shaving his beard.

What is it? What is it?

And then she sees.

She has no wrinkles.

Gran's face is as smooth as a child's, and her eyes shine a million times younger. It's as if time had suddenly punched out, all the years melting together into a tiny ball that got thrown out the window.

Suddenly Gran's laughter suits her face.

Gran notices Dani's lingering eyes. At first, she thinks that the girl is spacing off, but soon she realises that the girl is seeing. She's seeing something no one else can see.

"What is it, dear?" Gran whispers.

"It's your face…"

"My face? What about it?" Gran asks in a crescendoing whisper.

"It's young. You're young."

Gran lifts both hands and stretches her long aching fingers across the surface of her face. She feels the same old lines in the same old places, gashing her cheeks, lips and forehead. Same old downturned nose, same old soggy throat.

"You really see that?" Gran asks.

Dani only nods.

"I believe you," Gran admits fiercely.

Dani breaks her gaze and looks at Gran. Not the real Gran, but the Gran that is – the Gran that everyone can see. Suddenly her face is back to normal. Everything sags in all the right places and stretches downwards towards the ground.

"I think I'm a little bit of a witch," Dani says.

They look at each other for a long time.

Eventually, they both burst out laughing.

*

With only half an hour left before Gran has to leave for her lunch, Dani has time to read only one short metamorphosis. It's the story of a blind prophet, and how he came to be. His name was Tiresias (which rings a bell in Dani's mind. Not one that can be placed, and yet one that you can hear). It went like so:

The god Jupiter and his wife Juno (In Greek mythology known as Zeus and Hera) were having a spat. Jupiter claimed that women enjoy intercourse more than men, and Juno full-heartedly disagreed. So, to settle their argument, they asked Tiresias to weigh in. They had asked him because he had been both a man and a woman. This is the story of how that came to be:

Tiresias once saw two snakes mating in the forest. He decided to hit the snakes (as one decides to do) with a stick, and at that moment; he magically became a woman.

She lived as a woman for seven years. During the eighth year, she saw the snakes again and decided to hit them once more (because why not, right?). Tiresias immediately turned back into the gender in which he was born.

Thus, Tiresias had experienced all the pleasures of the world and had the answer which could settle Jupiter and Juno's little bet.

Tiresias confirmed Jupiter's claim.

Juno was furious. She swept an infinite night over Tiresias's eyes (aka blinded the poor guy).

Since no God can alter or cancel the makings of another God, Jupiter could not bring back his sight. Instead, he gave Tiresias the ability to see what the future holds. That way, Jupiter managed to relieve some weight from the heavy burden of blindness.

*

While Dani was reading the metamorphosis out loud, both Gran and herself could see it all play out in front of their eyes.

They could see the forest and the intertwined snakes. They could see Juno, ferociously beautiful, her lips stretched into a deep grimace filled with contempt and her eyes coloured a murky shade of revenge. They could see the light drain out of Tiresias's eyes.

Suddenly Dani wasn't alone in her visions. Both Gran and herself saw everything play out in front of them like a movie. For a few minutes, the eyes of their realities were one. It was refreshing and comforting at once.

Dani was enjoying the shared vision. Each word out of her mouth tasted like dessert, and she let them linger, soaking in the moment until it left.

*

After the metamorphosis, Gran goes out to lunch. Dani finishes cutting the fruit salad, wraps it up and slides it into the fridge. While the fridge door is still open, she inspects the contents of the shelves, scouring for lunch options. The fridge is almost completely filled to the brim, but unfortunately the only thing Dani is craving at the moment is minute-made noodle soup. The poison soup that's bad for your health, but good for your heart of hearts.

Dani's out the door and walking absently through the streets. There's a kind afternoon breeze coming up from the sea. The sidewalk is filled with people, and the street is packed with cars and an overwhelming amount of suicidal cyclists, swerving their way around and in front of the vehicles on the road. Dani lets her legs decide the way while her head is floating way above, barely connected to the rest of her body.

When she gets to the closest kiosk, she passes through the aisles rapidly, her eyes scanning all the shelves at once. She finds the minute-made noodle soup, grabs one from the very top of the stack (because everyone knows that the bottom ones are at the highest risk of getting corroded by shelf bugs) and goes straight to the front counter. She puts down the soup bowl – which barely gets away with being a Styrofoam cup – and rummages around her wallet for a ten-piece.

"You know that stuff is poison," a voice above her says.

Dani looks up to see the green-haired girl from last time.

Immediately, a fresh trail of strawberry sunrise marks her face from one cheek to the other. It takes her a second to get a hold of herself.

An awkward chuckle and a half later she comes up with, "They say that what doesn't kill you makes you stronger."

The girl with the green hair laughs.

"Then they've never had minute-made soup before," the girl says, and Dani laughs – almost comfortably. The girl with the green hair scans the soup and Dani hands her the money. The girl is about to give Dani her change when she suddenly pauses and pulls her hand back to her side.

"I remember you," she says. "You're the girl with the big eyes. From the other day, right?"

Dani's decorative trail of sunrise morphs into a full-body ordeal. Currently, it looks more like a rash than a tender rush of shyness.

"I guess," Dani manages. "And you're the girl with the green hair."

The girl with the green hair smiles a large, unbelievably crooked smile. It's so crooked that it seems physically impossible to smile so without unhinging a jaw. All of her teeth had visibly been straightened, and yet they seem out of order somehow. A Cheshire smile, wicked but kind.

The green-haired girl hands Dani the change once again. Dani holds out her hand to accept it, and before she has the time to pull away, the green-haired girl has wrapped her hand around hers. She squeezes tightly and shakes, while the coins rattle in between their joined grip.

"I'm Joey," she says.

"I'm Dani."

"Short for Daniel?"

"Yeah, but nobody calls me that."

"I like the name Daniel," the girl says factually. Here they both pause. What more can be said? Only half a second passes before Joey speaks again, but it's half a second spent standing in front of an abyss.

"I finish my shift in five minutes."

"Cool," Dani says, helplessly trying to reach for the right thing to say. Yet somehow when you need it the most, it's way out there – sometimes not even in sight.

"Yeah, cool," Joey teases kindly. "If you want to wait we can eat lunch together."

Dani feels almost shoved by Joey's forwardness. A shove as harsh as a blow to the jaw.

"Yes, sure, yes," Dani mumbles. Her tongue is burning up inside her throat, while her mind helplessly tries to hose it down.

*

Dani spends those five minutes sitting outside of the kiosk on a lonely street bench. She does absolutely nothing, and even this nothingness her body can hardly contain. She wants to scream, she wants to jump, she wants to run away. She doesn't even know this girl, but what was she supposed to do? Perhaps she could have come up with a lie about being in a hurry to get somewhere… but unfortunately, reasonable excuses don't come instinctively, and least of all on time.

After five minutes on the clock, and five decades in the heart, Joey comes out of the kiosk with a cup of minute-made noodle soup cupped between her hands.

"Sorry you had to wait," she says, "I hope it's okay that I asked you out."

"Asked me out… yes, okay, it's okay." Dani tries to morph her thoughts into coherent sentences. "Yes, I was free, all good."

Joey laughs.

This girl sure does laugh a lot. And she's also…

Floating. Joey is floating a few inches above the ground. She has on a black skirt with printed lemons scattered all over, their bright yellow glow shining like stars inside their black fabric world. The skirt is dancing wildly from the undetectable breeze of this hot, still, summer day.

Dani doesn't dare say a word.

They start walking aimlessly through the streets, simply talking, heading nowhere. Dani learns that Joey is only a year older. She takes one class at the university – oceanology, and the rest of the time she works at the kiosk in order to afford living in the city. She lives with two roommates, who are lovely people, and she doesn't know what she wants to do with her life. She likes green, but also pink. She tried to be a vegetarian but she missed her mom's meatballs too much. She never eats fish. She says they feel:

"Too fishy, you know?"

Dani doesn't know, but she finds it charming anyways.

After around fifteen minutes of wandering around, the mother of all questions is finally asked, by none other than our very own Dani. "Where are we going?"

"I don't know. I didn't really think this through."

Dani considers one possibility. Then she tosses it, and yet somehow it comes straight out of her mouth, "We can go eat the soup at my place – at my Gran's place. I live with my Gran."

Dani leads, and Joey follows. In the corner of her eyes, Dani can see that their shoulders are perfectly aligned – they must be almost the same height. Yet, every time that Dani looks over at Joey's face, Joey suddenly rises into the air and their shoulders disconnect. Dani tries to force herself to keep her eyes forward, but the green hair demands to be looked at, at least every once in a while.

So she steals a few glances. She takes in the green hair flying around the humid air, and the green eyes that completely pop out of her profile, almost more so than her nose. They look like large jello shots, and their effect is every bit as intoxicating. She can't stop looking, and with every look, she gets hungrier and hungrier to steal another. It becomes this kind of game, almost like she's daring herself to look again and again, stretching the limits, trying to find out when the line will be crossed.

"You know that I can see you, right?" Joey suddenly says.

"Even if I don't turn my eyes towards you. I think it's called peripheral vision?" She turns her head to look at Dani and flashes her the silliest, most crooked half-smile that she had ever seen in her entire life.

Dani only blushes. That seems to be her response to most – if not all – of the things that come out of Joey's mouth.

"Peripheral vision, yeah," Dani says, almost in a whisper. "I don't think they taught us that at my high school."

Joey bursts out laughing.

Maybe I'm creepy, but at least I'm funny I guess.

Dani's joke riles up another wave of conversation. Dani learns that Joey's best friends are, in fact, her roommates. Joey says that rent isn't too bad in their part of the city, and that after splitting the rent, bills, food and other basics between three people you still have some money to spend. She says that she always saves up the money, and then spends it all in one place – about once every two months.

"Where do you spend all the money? Do you just go to the mall once every two months and go nuts? That actually sounds really fun."

Joey doesn't answer. For the first time since they've met, Dani can sense an air of uneasiness swirling around her. She looks over at her, and the first thing she notices is how she lifts into the air – but that is to be expected by now. The surprise is stemmed from seeing a field of cranberries slowly growing out of her cheeks and the bridge of her nose. Real, round, burning red cranberries.

Usually blushing is enough indication of someone's heart, but apparently not now.

Now there's a cranberry field in full bloom blotting Joey's

pale face.

Why cranberries? Why isn't blushing enough?

Usually blushing is bittersweet, but cranberries are sour.

She's ashamed.

"Not exactly," Joey says. "I always spend it on… It's just that, you see…"

"You don't have to tell me," Dani cuts her off. "It's fine. You don't owe me any explanations."

Joey turns her head to look at Dani. She is no longer embellished by a wild trail of cranberries – now she is simply red. She's not blushing, at least not in the sweet sense of it. She's angry. Her reddening face clashes horribly with the green fringe falling gracefully over her brows.

"I know I don't owe you anything. Don't worry, I don't speak unless I want to."

"Yeah of course. I'm sorry," Dani blurts out.

They walk in silence for the next few minutes. Dani doesn't know what to say. She doesn't completely understand what had just happened. She can't seem to track down the root of the tension.

Poor girl – Dani has yet to learn that emotions come out of everything, and in some cases out of nothing that only seems like everything. Emotions are pure creations; why, they are the art that every single one of us can uphold.

"I spend it all on skydiving," Joey says suddenly.

Dani is shocked enough to snap out of her confusion. She immediately wants to know more. She wants to get down to the root of such a strange habit. However, the best that Joey can offer as an explanation is this; because 'it makes her happy'.

Because it makes you happy?

"Because it makes me happy. Yeah. Honestly, I can't think of another reason."

"Because it makes you happy?" Dani repeats.

Joey laughs and turns to her.

"Why is that so surprising? Almost everything I do is for that reason."

"So you work at the kiosk because it makes you happy?" Dani doesn't wait for her to answer. "Of course not! You work there because you need the money to pay for food, clothes and rent!"

Joey's laugh only grows stronger in response to Dani's disbelief.

"Yeah, I guess that's true. But I still like it. I get a lot of free snacks, and I talk to tons of different people every day. And every once in a while I meet someone really cool," Joey says and winks at Dani.

Dani crumbles. She can taste the disintegrated bones melting in her mouth. They're sweet.

The two girls walking side by side finally turn onto Dani's street. Before they reach the building, Dani feels just one more question rising inside her gut. She lets loose – *what the hell, right?*

"OK, I just have to ask."

Joey turns her large green eyes to Dani.

"Why do you colour your hair green?"

"What, don't you like it?" Joey asks, almost flirtatiously.

"No, no, that's not it," Dani stumbles on her words. "I guess I was just wondering. I um, forget it, really."

Joey truly can't seem to stop laughing.

"I'm just playing with you!" Joey playfully elbows Dani in the shoulder. "It's kind of embarrassing really. The truth, I mean. I guess I could lie but I figure – what the hell, right?"

Dani immediately shifts her gaze towards Joey's eyes. Underneath them is a rosy hue, making her even more beautiful than before, if such a thing could be.

"I guess I colour my hair because it makes me feel… special, I guess."

"Why is that embarrassing? I don't think that's embarrassing," Dani says, her eyes still locked on Joey. Now she's tracing Joey's long green hair with her eyes; the thin strings of green falling onto her forehead and almost into her eyes. Those eyes that unbelievably nearly match the electric green colour of her hair.

"I guess it's embarrassing because of how much I care. About being special I mean."

Dani doesn't know what to say to this confession. It makes her like Joey even more.

*

The second they enter through the apartment door, Gran leaps up on Dani and begins showing all the new patches she's embroidered in the past few days. Dani identifies the patch with a daffodil, and another with two intermingled snakes. She recognises a few other metamorphoses that they've read together, but most of the patches hold stories she's never heard of before. Gran explains that she simply could not wait, so she continued embroidering stories that they have yet to read.

Only after Dani has commented on every single one of the patches does Gran notice Joey standing beside her, a little ways behind. Dani introduces them to each other and the two of them shake hands politely. Dani could swear that for a second their hands had morphed into two halves of a whole, like puzzle pieces perfectly lining up with one another. If nothing else, it was an indication of the instant connection that followed.

Apparently, Joey had not only heard about Ovid's metamorphoses, but she had already read it. Not as trivial as one might think, and yet Gran seemed to think of it not only as a good sign but as a nameless destiny. Gran simply could not shut her mouth, and the questions came blurting out like vomit: When? How? Why? Where?

Suddenly Gran not only wanted to know everything about Joey's 'Metamorphoses' reading experience, but also everything else about her. Dani would have stopped Gran short, yet her curiosity for hearing Joey's answers dissipated any type of resistance. Also, to be as fair as fair can be, Gran's questions were pretty fucking great. In another life Gran could have been a psychologist, or even some sort of a detective.

Now they were talking about Joey's skirts. Apparently, she wears only skirts – pants are too restricting for her taste. She likes the skirts long and powerfully coloured. Joey says that she picks the skirt according to the way she wants to feel that particular day.

"But why would you want to feel anything other than happy?" Dani asks, and without her noticing Gran rolls her eyes.

Joey, on the other hand, answers sweetly, "Sometimes

sadness is too close to resist. Or, um, sometimes you're so lonely that even loneliness feels like a friend, you know?"

Dani thought that perhaps she did know, though she wasn't quite sure. She had never been swallowed whole by a feeling, neither happiness nor otherwise. She has felt, as we all have. She has even cried, screamed and run around in ecstasy. Yet feelings have always walked along with her hand in hand, never stepping out of line with her, never overstepping through the personal bubble of her comfort. Dani has never lived inside an ocean, slowly drowning away. Oh, she has known some tough times, but no tougher than falling from your bike and scratching your knee. Dani has never known what broken bone times felt like, and never known how broken heart times ached.

Even now, as the three of them sit across from each other on the bar stools, Dani can see Joey floating above the chair, her long skirt is fluttering about from the still, standing air of the indoors.

"Does it work?" Dani asks all of a sudden.

"Does what work?" Joey asks.

"Picking out skirts according to what you want to feel. Does it actually work?"

"Sure it does, child," Gran answers, and Joey reinforces by saying:

"If you believe it does."

"And you believe it does?" Dani asks.

Joey looks at her with cross eyes and a fresh flush in her cheeks.

"Of course I do." She answers with such an air of confidence that Dani feels ashamed for having even asked.

"Besides, wearing skirts reminds me of skydiving. Sometimes when the wind is just right, and my skirt keeps brushing against my ankles, again and again… It almost feels like I'm flying. It's like, I get so focused on the skirt brushing up against my ankles that I almost seem to forget that I have feet. And if I have no feet, well then, I'm never on the ground."

*

Joey stays until it's time for dinner. Gran insists that she stay, but Joey doesn't want to impose. Dani, as much as she wanted Joey to stay, was at the same time quite relieved by her departure.

Good. It would be dangerous to fall in love too quickly, she thinks.

Dani attends to making dinner. As she's chopping potatoes, her face turned away from Gran, she rustles up the courage to ask, "Did you notice anything unusual about Joey?"

Gran immediately stops her embroidering.

"What do you mean?"

"Never mind. If you don't know then you just didn't see."

"What did *you* see?" Gran asks, unable to keep her childish curiosity from spilling through her words. It does no good; Dani detects it and her old (yet still not rusty) teenage instincts kick in and she says, "Forget it."

Now there's silence. Gran tries to grasp at it, and yet it keeps slipping through all the words left unsaid.

"I did…" Gran says, "I did see her skirt fluttering. I thought maybe it was some kind of draft, but I'm sitting in her chair right now, and I don't feel a damn thing, dearie."

Dani turns around to look at Gran, her eyes eating up her

face.

"Did you see anything else?"

"No, that's all I can think of."

There's a pause.

"Why? What did *you* see, dear?"

"I keep seeing her… hovering. Like, floating above the ground."

For the first time, Gran doesn't seem surprised at Dani's vision. She doesn't speak for a minute, but eventually, she says, "That quite suits her, now doesn't it? She's a special one."

9. Luca

Luca is walking out of the pharmacy. In her backpack, she has four cases of stretch gauze, two bottles of disinfectant spray and a large squeeze bottle of Neosporin.

She's exhausted from walking, she's exhausted from standing up, but the world doesn't stop because she tried to kill herself. No one around her knows that she could have been gone today, and no one cares. The world is just the same. She is so small, so unimportant.

The world keeps moving on, the days rapidly following one another like waves, and she has to keep swimming, or at least make it look like she is. It's as if everyone is riding on these waves, one after the other, but Luca has long ago dropped anchor. She's slowly fading beneath the waves, drowning, dying.

Luca suddenly sees Fred – the sappy sunfish – floating in front of her, mocking her with his wide glare.

"Get out of here, you bloated fillet," she orders him with a smirk.

Fred blows out an array of charmingly disfigured air bubbles.

Luca rolls her eyes, and then begins to roll them a second time, but stops halfway, keeping her pupils glued to the back of her lids. Her eyes squint, her brows curve towards one another and her forehead furrows in thought. She shoots another look towards Fred. Fred-the-sunfish. She reads the sign behind him. He's standing in front of an aquatic pet store.

It's so nice to see instead of feel. It's so nice to see instead of feel. It's so nice to see instead of feel!! It's so nice to see instead of feel!!!!

Suddenly, she has an idea. It springs remote energy inside her.

"Thanks, Fred, you're the man," Luca whispers, and even manages to shoot him a friendly wink.

*

DANIOS

MOLLY

PLATIES

TETRA

So many different types of seemingly brainless, colourful fish to choose from – and worst of all, so many decisions to make. Freshwater fish or saltwater fish, a round aquarium or a square aquarium, a miniature castle or a miniature pirate ship, colourful pebbles or no pebbles, betta fish or friendly fish… She's in way over her head.

Eventually, she settles on two tiny zebrafish in a square

aquarium and some aquamarine-coloured pebbles. She's quite satisfied with herself, her decisions and the amount of money she just threw away for something that she'll surely flush down the toilet in a month. She has just made a decision on a total whim, during a sleepless craze….

Her thoughts begin to spiral, but not too badly, for she's able to conclude that perhaps this was a bad idea. She looks down at her right hand holding the plastic bag, pregnant with water and air, trapping inside two hysterical fish swimming around wildly.

As she passes by a garbage bin on the side of the street, a slippery thought quickly glides through her mind. She could just throw the fish into the bin and it would all be over with. No fish, no problems. How silly it is that this sudden problem is one that she accumulated for herself, like a gift from her inner saboteur. All Luca wants to do at this moment is to trade in her worries for new, spotless, fresh out of the box misery. She could deal with pain as long as it was on a swift and never-ending cycle of metamorphosis.

She should throw the fish in the trash, yet she doesn't. She needs to do this. After all, getting out of the house and purchasing these possibly life-saving fish is a victory, a victory that she would not tarnish with her weak ways.

When Luca gets home, she cleans the square aquarium with a soapy sponge soaked with water until its glass walls are immaculate. She spills the aquamarine pebbles into the aquarium and fills it up with lukewarm water. Finally, she takes the plastic bag with the fish and places it inside of the aquarium water. She waits an hour for the water inside of the bag to reach the temperature of the water outside of it. Then, she releases the two zebrafish into their new home.

Watching the fish swim around freely inside those four glass walls, she feels contentment sink into her heart. She tries to convince this feeling to drop anchor, or at least to stay awhile, yet it does no such thing.

Quickly emptiness takes over – it's the nothingness that makes her hollow heart tick.

But even through the nothingness, she can see the fish.

These fish are real, she thinks to herself.

She lifts her head and takes a long look at the world around her. A normal human world submerged in the ocean of her mind. So many animals inhabit her ocean, and not even one of them is real. Her ocean isn't real. The only thing that's real is the two little zebrafish swimming around in the square bowl. They're real. They're the only thing that's real. They'll be her grasp.

Fred the sunfish; he isn't real. The purple octopus she sees in the corner of her eye, clinging onto a marron lamp standing beside her desk, he isn't real. All the parrotfish murking her vision, they're not real. But these zebrafish inside this bowl right here, they're real. Oh, they're very real.

She smiles. She will no longer be fooled.

"Luca, what is that?"

It's her sister.

"I bought fish," Luca answers simply.

"You bought fish," her sister repeats dubiously.

After a silent minute her sister gently asks, "Why… Why did you buy fish?"

What is Luca supposed to tell her? She had bought the fish because *they're real...* but how is the reality of something a qualified reason for its existence? What was she to say without sounding like a fool, or worse than that – a lunatic?

"I just wanted fish," Luca says with her head down.

"What did you say? Look at me when you speak!"

Luca raises her head to face her sister and repeats in a mumble, "I just wanted fish."

Her sister smacks her hand to her forehead. When she lifts her gaze, Luca can see that her eyes are rapidly beginning to overflow.

"How are you going to take care of fish? You can barely take care of yourself!" her sister yells.

"I just wanted fish... I just wanted FUCKING FISH!"

Now it's silent. It only keeps stretching out further and further. Luca doesn't look at her sister, and yet she can feel her gaze. Her sister probably thinks she has officially gone mad. If things weren't bad before, they'll be even worse now. Luca knows things will get worse, but all she can focus on is how horrific things seem to be right now. *It's just fish. You didn't do anything crazy, she tells* herself. She just wishes that this silence would end. Let them move on from these clenching minutes; she can't bear it any longer. She waits for her sister to speak, yet she doesn't.

Luca holds one end of the silence, her sister the other. No knife comes between it, and it never snaps. Eventually, her sister simply walks out of the room, stretching the silence behind her, tugging at Luca on the other end, never letting her rest. Luca can bear it no longer. There's nothing that can fix this now. It may only be silence to someone else, but to her, it's the end.

Luca looks over at her brand-new aquarium. It makes her

feel the slightest bit better. She watches the two zebrafish chase one another's tails. They go round and round, up and down, up and down, up and down, up and *out (?)*. The two fish start jumping out of the aquarium water and quickly fall back in with a splash.

What the hell are they doing? Luca thinks to herself, her heart suddenly beating in her ears.

The fish do it again. One after the other they jump out and fall back into the aquarium. They do it again. And again. And again. And on the sixth jump, they never fall back in. They fly out of the aquarium and start floating above it, swerving their bodies wildly.

After a few seconds of confusion, the fish come to their senses and start swimming around regularly. They swim to Luca's bookshelf, rub themselves against her bed, race each other around the light of her lamp and eventually find their way out of her window and into the street.

Luca looks down at her empty aquarium.

Nothing good lasts in my world.

She has officially lost her grip. Her last grip. There's nothing left to do, nothing left to give. She's no longer drowning… she has drowned.

Before she realises what she's doing, she finds herself walking through the streets of Telo like a ghost.

A minute later, she's standing on a sandy strip of beach.

In seconds, she's in the ocean, the salty water all the way up to her shoulders. She knows it's a real ocean because her eyes can see its surface – this ocean has a beginning, and an end.

Her eyes are almost level with the surface.

Then, she's underwater, as usual, but now she can't breathe.

10. Dani

They're sitting together on a small grassy hill in the middle of the park. For the first time, they're hand in hand. It's nice. It's sweet. The feelings creep up into Dani's throat and demand to be released, but all she can do for them is a smile. Maybe that's good enough. No, it's *great*.

"I wish I could fly," Joey says out of the blue.

Swept up in her feelings, Dani answers without thinking, "Maybe you already can."

Joey turns to look at her. A curious smile is on her lips, so bent and wonderful.

"Do you really think so?"

"I really do."

It's quiet, but the silence is accompanied by the afternoon breeze whispering through their hair. They don't speak, but the children playing next by are laughing, intoxicating the air.

"No one's ever told me that before," Joey says.

"That's bad. Especially considering the fact that all you really want to do is fly."

Joey's kissing her. It's out of nowhere, and yet right now – in these seconds – it's everything.

"Thank you," Joey says.

"For what?"

"For helping me fly."

"But I didn't do anything."

"You believed I could."

So far, Joey and herself have never talked about being together forever, and yet somewhere inside their minds they had made an agreement at this very moment. It was a secret thing, but a sure thing, and it was comforting, and good.

*

"Hey, Gran," Dani says as she walks through the door.

"Hello, dearie. Look at this new patch I just finished embroidering."

The patch shows a miniature man and woman sitting inside a small boat.

"Deucalion and Pyrrha?"

"Yes, of course."

*

The purification of mankind: In Ovid's mind the world was flooded by the tears of Jupiter. Every animal and human was drowned, that is except for Deucalion and Pyrrha. Deucalion and Pyrrha were perfect. whatever that means.

"They were perfect in the eyes of the gods." Gran had said, back when they were reading this metamorphosis.

The only animals left alive after the flood were the ones which had the ability to breathe underwater. The world was picturesque; dolphins rubbing their backs on the tops of oak trees, the bellies of ships scraping the roofs of castles and anchors ploughing sunken plains.

Despite the beauty, Deucalion and Pyrrha were greatly upset. The god Hermes decided to take pity on them, so he gave them a clue as to how to rebuild the human world as it once was. "You must throw the bones of your mother over your shoulders."

Deucalion and Pyrrha were confused by his words, but eventually, half-heartedly agreed that 'bones' must be stones, and their 'mother' must be the Earth. So, they picked up all the stones they could find, and one by one they threw them over their shoulders.

Lo and behold, all the stones turned into human beings; the ones thrown by Pyrrha became women, and the ones thrown by Deucalion became men.

*

"Yeah, I remember reading about them," Dani says. "These are the two that just took a wild guess at a half-assed prophecy, and it worked on the first try."

"You know, dearie," Gran answers, unbothered by Dani's tone of voice, "some things have an urgent nature. Some things simply must come to pass. Whether it be Hermes' prophecy that you refer to as being – oh dear lord – 'half-assed'… or be it Joey's belief in her skirts, which is a full-hearted deal."

Dani doesn't know what to say.

"What I'm trying to say is that sometimes you must use

your gut, child, and you must have the guts to try, because life has a way of surprising you."

Without knowing exactly what Gran is blabbing about, Dani can feel a seed implanted deep in the back of her mind.

"I believe life will surprise you, dearie. I do. I believe you will surprise yourself. Oh, lords be it – I believe in *you*."

She believes. In me… amongst other things. She believes in the urgent nature of the world.

"Gran, I need you to do something for me," The words slip out of Dani's mouth as if it weren't her own. Her instincts have kicked in, and her lips move automatically. "I need you to make more metamorphoses patches. A lot more. And I don't want a blanket. I need you to make me a skirt."

11. Luca

Luca opens her eyes to the unbearable brightness of the light seeping in through the open window. For a split-second, the light feels like a new beginning.

Trickery – that's what it is. When she blinks the world comes back into view. The world as the world truly is. An ocean. An abyss, hopeless and large.

She's in a hospital bed. She's in the hospital, she realises. The room is sterile, white and empty, except for herself and a long plastic tube hanging between a bag of IV fluid and her wrist. From her chest down she is covered in a white linen blanket. She tries not to think about all the ones who have laid under it before herself.

Luca's alone in the room, until she's not. A nurse steps into the room and asks her how she feels. A rather unhistoric interaction.

Later, her sister comes in and sits beside her, visibly fighting back the tears. This feels familiar but rotten, like an apple with a hidden worm. To the naked eye the apple seems quite fine, normal. Yet Luca can sense the worm making its way through the apple, tearing it apart from the inside. She can feel the worm pulsing inside her veins, denying her every part of the apple.

*

Luca's loneliness truly shatters when Ms. Porcelain comes in.

Even in her state, Luca finds herself so shocked that she can't speak. Even after death, life still manages to surprise.

Ms. Porcelain doesn't say anything. She simply sits down in the chair beside Luca's bed. They don't speak, they don't even acknowledge one another with eye contact. They know enough – perhaps too much. Luca knows that Ms. Porcelain is there. She never questions it, never once moves her eyes to check. She's there. She's there, and that's good enough.

They stay silent for a long while, time slowly slipping through their fingers like sand, slowly floating back down to the ocean floor and joining the sandy bottom, too immense and stretched out to count, or even consider.

The sleeping time overshadows actions, and suddenly Ms. Porcelain's hand is on her own. It's warm and real. It's underwater like hers. Ms. Porcelain isn't reaching from above. She's not trying to pull her back up; she's no advocate for the beachy strip waiting just outside.

Ms. Porcelain is sitting down on the ocean floor right beside her, holding her hand. She isn't drowning, she has lots of air left in her lungs, so she allows herself to stay a while longer, right beside Luca, holding her hand.

The silence takes up the entirety of Ms. Porcelain's visit. Right as she stands up to leave, she swiftly replaces the weight of her hand with another. It's foreign and cold to the touch.

As Ms. Porcelain stands in the doorframe looking back, Luca's eyes travel down to her hand. It's a book. On its cover is written in big bold letters:

Metamorphoses
By Ovid

"A little gift," Ms. Porcelain says, and Luca lifts her eyes to look back at her. The morning light coming in through the window warms up her pale face, and Luca can clearly see every beige freckle glowing in the warmth. Her eyes are large, and her lips are coloured a light pink; she looks almost gorgeous.

She walks out without waiting for a reply.

Good, Luca thinks. *I wouldn't have been able to think of one even if I truly tried.*

Luca opens the front cover of the book to see a pen inscribed message:

To Luca,
I hope you know that I truly care.
From Dani

*

Luca spends the entirety of her stay at the hospital reading the stories inside the book. She barely notices as Fred the sunfish comes creeping into her room and leans awkwardly on the back wall.

One metamorphosis somehow seeps in deeper than the rest. It's one of the shortest and most forgettable tales in the book, and yet, despite its nature (or perhaps because of it), it managed to slip into her heart without wrinkling it.

It tells the story of a young couple who's told that they will not be allowed to have a daughter. If their child was born female, she was to be slaughtered.

However, while the soon-to-be mother was sleeping, a goddess came to her through the shutter of a dream and told her to raise her future daughter as if she were a boy.

So she did.

After many years of growing up, it came time for the girl disguised as a man to marry. Since she was presenting herself as male, her future was to be shared with a woman.

The match was made, and slowly the girl found herself falling in love with her bride. She didn't know how such a thing could come to be; she's a girl, and it's a girl her heart desires!

Disaster was awaiting. Yet, just as our female groom was walking down the aisle, she was transformed into a man by the mercy of one of the gods.

Luca didn't quite understand the big fuss over being a lesbian, but she realised that this was a different time.

The fact that stuck in her mind was the miracle. At that time, the only thing to save the situation was a metamorphosis. For some reason, this stuck in her mind like gum to the sidewalk. Eventually, after much consideration, it became a dark spot stuck tightly onto the makings of her mind. A key to the cementing of her conscious.

M-e-t-a-m-o-r-p-h-o-s-e-s. The word lingered while she ate her hospital meals. The word smoothly tethered her dreams to one another at night, and in the morning it was the first thing that passed through her waking mind.

At last, the reason became apparent.

12. Dani

"It's done."

"What is?" Dani asks.

"The skirt," Gran answers hastily. "It's done."

"I'm going to call Joey right now; can you believe she doesn't know anything about this? It's been so hard keeping it a secret!"

"Well, dearie, I'm——" -

"Joey? Hello?" Dani's already on the phone. "Meet me at the park in half an hour." -

"Oh, alright, then when do you get off?" -

"Okay so I'll see you then."

*

Dani's sitting on their usual grassy hill in the park, music blasting from her Sony headphones, her right hand gripped tightly onto the handles of a brown paper bag sitting beside her.

Suddenly, her left earphone is pulled out of her ear. She looks up, startled, to see Joey holding the earphone in her hand. Dani's tightly strung face relaxes as if on cue.

"Hey," Dani says.

"Hey to you too."

"I have something for you."

"Really? What for?"

"Doesn't matter," Dani hands her the brown paper bag. "Just open it."

Joey sits down on the grass next to Dani and takes the bag out of her hand. A meandering smile colours her face with joy. She looks directly at Dani as she pulls the skirt out of the bag.

"Oh my god. Is this what I think it is?"

"It's a metamorphoses skirt."

Joey gently runs her fingers along the patches covering the entirety of the skirt.

"I have to try it on," she says. "Like, right now!"

She puts on the metamorphoses skirt over the skirt she's already wearing. The waistband of the metamorphoses skirt snaps over her hips, and slides onto her waist like a glove. Then she pulls the first skirt from underneath the metamorphoses skirt and flings it to the ground.

"I can't believe it. It's perfect. It's perfect!" She kneels down onto the grass and gives Dani a kiss.

Then Joey springs back up and begins twirling in place, allowing the skirt to flutter all around her long legs. Only her ankles show once every few seconds as the skirt is lifted by the wind.

She doesn't stop spinning. In Dani's eyes she only raises higher and higher into the air, every spin granting her more freedom. The higher up she goes the wider the view of the world must be. She can probably see everything so clearly from up there. Everyone else must look so small, so still; infantile creatures of this earth claiming their place under the sun.

"I'm flying! I can feel it!" Joey yells with her eyes closed. "I'm flying I swear! I'm going to open my eyes, and from that moment on I will never walk on the ground again!"

A shiver so strong – almost painful even – runs down Dani's back. She doesn't need her eyes, or even her special kind of vision to realise that something's about to change. Not for the worst, and probably for the better, yet the powerful blow of change is undeniable. It's one of the scariest hurdles of this world. A large part of what makes it so frightening is the fact that it must always come. Again, and again, never truly letting us live in peace, never letting us wilt away from sitting still.

Joey opens her eyes to the world, not for the first time and not for the last. Somewhere in the midst of her life she opens her eyes, a flutter of the lid placed between all the flutters before, and all the flutters yet to come. Joey opens her eyes to the sky, but for the first time in doing so, no part of her is on the ground. A feeling so bright it threatens to overwhelm rushes through her. A sensation of light and weightlessness. Joey looks down at her feet, trying to make sense of the sensation. How did she not notice it before?

There's no denying it now. Her feet are off the ground. Her eyes cannot lie. There is Dani, down below. So small, yet clearly there, standing her ground. If Dani's all the way down there, then she must really be all the way...

"Is this really happening??" Joey screams from above.

"What do you think?!" Dani yells to the sky, her hands covering her eyes from the sun.

"I think I'm flying!!"

She really is, Dani thinks. *And I had something to do with that.*

A warm wave sweeps her insides – a light shining from within.

What is this feeling? Pride? Accomplishment?

I wish it could last forever… Or at the very least, come again and again.

"Dani!! Look! I'm flying!!"

Dani smiles up at Joey. She's up in the sky, her skirt fluttering, morphing, changing into the shape of the wind.

I knew you could fly. I already knew.

I saw it before anyone else – even before you.

I'm so glad you can see it now too.

If I can help you fly, what else can I do?

13. Luca

It's her fifth day in the hospital. They say her condition has stabilised. Tomorrow she'll be moved to the psych ward.

It's nighttime, and her room is dark and still. From the small square window on the door, a faint light manages to slip in from the neon bulbs out in the hall. Every once in a while Luca can hear the soft shuffle of a doctor passing by, or stifled laughter coming from the nurse's station at the end of the hall.

They're going to admit me to the psych ward, but it's only because they don't know what I know, she thinks.

Sitting up in bed, with a blanket wrapped around her lower section, Luca raises the blanket with one hand and peers underneath to look at the bottom half of herself. It's the same as before.

Slimy, scaled and ocean-blue. Long, going all the way to the very tip of the bed. Whole, until it splits in two at the bottom. That's what her tail looks like. She can flap the end of it at the very least, and barely lift the whole of it at the very most. It's as if the air isn't quite strong enough to bear the tail, as if gravity is too overbearing. Either way, she's not in the right place.

Luca presses the metamorphoses book tightly to her chest. She stays that way as she drifts off to sleep.

14. Dani

Dani presses the code for the front door, and as the buzzer sounds, she opens the door and steps inside. Just as she begins walking up the stairs, her phone rings, so she takes it out of her small pleather backpack, and when the screen lights on from her touch she sees a text from Joey that reads:

Good luck on your first day in the new office!

A smile spreads on her face at the thought of Joey. Yet even with a smile on her face, she can't help but fret. She had only been inside this office once, and that had been the same day that she signed the lease. There was definitely a time constraint in regards to finding a new office space, that's for sure. With Gran selling her house and moving into the spare room in the apartment owned by Joey and herself, there was already enough to do in her spare time, and not much was left for finding a new space to work. Also, the truth of the matter is that she was putting off the search. It's not that she wasn't glad that Gran was moving in with them instead of going to some nursing home, but deep inside she did kind of hate giving up the room she used as her office. She liked seeing her patients inside her own home, and not only that, she thought her patients seemed to like it just as much. It's more personal, more humane. The least she could do to thank them for letting her inside their world is to welcome them inside her home and help themselves to a cup of tea – with sugar or without? Also her wife had just made some cookies the other night, would you like to try one? They're truly the best. Feel free to put your legs up on the couch, and there's a blanket if you want. Really, make yourself at home.

Home. Exactly the opposite of the office in front of her now; white, bare. *Sterile* is the word that comes to mind, from the plastic cups beside the water cooler to the white noise machine standing next to the glass candy bowl. The first thing she does is quickly rush over to the white noise machine and try to turn it off. She presses every button she can find – for Christ sake, she even pulls its wire out of the plug on the wall – but even after all that, the stupid machine won't give up.

"Well, you are just white noise after all…" She lifts the machine and places it behind the large candy jar that's filled almost all the way up to the top. "So if we can't see you, it's like you don't even exist." With these words comes the thought of Gran.

She smiles as she takes a Jolly Rancher out of the candy bowl. She pops it into her mouth as she unlocks the door to the inner office.

"Gosh, how dull," she says as she pulls the door open, the Jolly Rancher dancing on her tongue. The room is no different than its predecessor. She closes the door behind her and inspects; the only notable thing inside is a large picture of

Telo hung on the wall just over the chair in front of her. She walks towards it and places her bag beside the chair.

She sits in the chair for a while, nonsensically chatting with Joey through texts, until she realises the time and gets up to walk out of the room, determined to make herself a decent cup of coffee before her first patient arrives. She opens the door slowly, still looking down at her phone, and just as she steps out the door and into the outer waiting room, she sees her. No, that's not exactly accurate. She sees the girl – she does – but the first thing that truly catches her eye is everything *around* her.

Never before had she seen someone who carried *so much* with them. She had seen people distorted in many ways by their emotions, but never to this extent. This girl… this strange, unfamiliar girl has an entire ocean surrounding her. Dani can clearly see the body of water encompassing her entirely. She doesn't know why the word 'ocean' immediately came to mind, because water by itself doesn't necessarily mean an ocean; usually an ocean is classified as one by the life force existing within it. Yet the body of water around this girl is so clearly an ocean, despite being bare. It's something in the way that the water moves, as if it's sighing heavily... and it's the colour, it's definitely the colour that gives it away. No body of water but an ocean has a colour like that; that deep, aching cerulean, empty of all humanity and yet so clearly alive. That blue that only an ocean can achieve.

Dani realises that she must do something other than stare at the poor girl. She cracks a fake smile, agonising over trying to remember her name. This girl is a first-time patient, and never before had she been caught so completely off guard during the job. This is not a good start.

"Hello," Dani says in her most assertive tone, sure that the sound of her own voice will force her back into her skin. Sure enough, the name of the girl quickly realises in her memory. "Luca?"

"Yes," The girl answers shortly. It's a soft, tender voice, almost waiting to be broken.

"Come on in," Dani says and gestures for Luca to come inside the inner room.

After they've settled down into their chairs, Dani begins her regular 'first meeting' speech. She tells Luca her name, her profession – as if she doesn't already know – and she mentions that she's married to a wonderful woman. The girl in front of her doesn't seem to be paying attention, not even one bit, and yet Dani keeps going, because, over the years, this speech has become more than a formality; it has become somewhat of a superstitious habit. If she starts, she must finish it to the end in one go. A little superstition never hurts.

"So that's a little bit about me."

The girl doesn't reply. Dani quickly picks up the conversation stick before it falls on the floor. "It's nice to finally meet you."

"Yeah," is all the girl says to that.

"Tell me a little bit about yourself." Dani places both hands on the stick. This is a two-man job.

"I'm 17. I dropped out of school. You're my fifth psychologist in the last year," Luca blurts out as if this had been rehearsed.

No, not rehearsed. It's just been said time and time again. Poor girl.
And now there's silence. There's no mistaking it.

"I can see that this is hard for you." Dani lifts the stick with all her might.

"Yeah. I'm tired," Luca blurts.

Ouch. The 'I'm tired' excuse is the most painful one of all. Particularly because it's true – she is tired. But the real problem isn't her exhaustion, the problem is all that's causing it.

The rest of the meeting inches on second by second. Nothing gets done, nothing of importance gets said. Not the most hopeful first session Dani has ever run, but still, it's a start nonetheless. At the very least, by the end of the meeting Dani is certain; this girl isn't surrounded by an ocean – she's *drowning* inside one.

15. Luca and Dani

The world outside the car window is a view for the gods. The sun has just begun to rise, highlighting the ocean and colouring the sky with every shade between pink and orange. They're the only car on the road heading down to the beach. The road below is blurred by their speed, but the view ahead sits still, promising to wait for their arrival. With every minute that passes, the sun reflects more and more stars onto the waves, twinkling and flirting with the tide.

Dani turns to look at Luca sitting in the back seat. Her forehead is leaned on the glass, and her eyes are far away. She seems calm and in control, despite floating into the view. She turns her eyes back to the road, and as she does, Joey's hand slips into her own.

She's wearing her metamorphoses skirt today, Dani thinks. *Everything is alright.*

It had been a month since Luca tried to slip away. Just this morning she was released from the psychiatric ward of the hospital. It's a new beginning – they'll make sure of it. Everything is already different after all; Luca got a new therapist while at the hospital, whom she seems to get along with, and as for Luca and herself – they had gone through a metamorphosis, if you will. They became something new, almost like a family, it seems.

At last they make it to the beach. Their feet slip into the sand, hot at the surface and chilled right below. Dani is holding Luca in her arms, one hand on her back and the other at the centre of her tail. She takes her right to the wavering seam of the ocean and sand, and there she places her on the damp, hard ground. She places a hand on the top of Luca's head and smiles at her kindly.

"Go to her," Luca says. "I'll be fine."

Dani nods in agreement. "I know you will." She glides her hand off Luca's head and offers another gentle smile, yet this time it's glazed with fear.

Luca nods as if to say, 'I promise. Trust me.'

Dani doesn't dare betray that offer. She nods in return, even though her heart is filled with doubt.

It's the burden of loving someone of the sea.

Luca watches as Dani makes her way towards Joey, who's already sitting on a blanket she spread out on the sand. Luca watches as the morning sun reflects off of Dani's porcelain skin, not a single ray managing to soak through her fair exterior. Only the freckles all over her body are a testament to her shortcomings.

She turns to look at the ocean.

It's time to jump in.

She hadn't seen the insides of an ocean for a long time now, almost over a month. Ever since the tail came to be, the ocean disappeared. Not completely, for sometimes she still saw Fred The Sunfish wandering about, but for the most part the ocean had retreated. Where had it gone? She didn't really wish to know. For some reason she had a feeling that the answer won't bring her any relief, so why bother trying to find out?

Luca waits for the next wave to come, and when it finally does, she allows herself to be washed up by its force. When the wave retreats back into the depths, so does she, and soon she's already under the waves, hearing them crash from above. She swims deeper, and deeper, never needing to come up for air.

The deeper she goes the more she sees. In the depths lie all kinds of life, out of reach for anyone but herself. The deeper she goes the more comfortable she is inside her own skin, her new form. The deeper she goes the farther her own ocean seems to be. She has finally found something worth living for. She has finally found a place where she belongs. Through Dani, and herself, she managed to make the worst time of her life into a spring for a new beginning. She launched herself into the ocean. It may not be for everyone, but that's what makes it her very own way.

This she can do. She really can swim. So what if she fell off the boat and everyone kept on sailing without her? She managed to free her own anchor, and learned to swim. Now she's a better swimmer than them all – just look at her go!

She's cutting through the water at frightening speed. Fearless, she passes by a manta ray that had been heading rapidly towards her path. She cracks a smile, and thousands of tiny bubbles come rushing out of her mouth. She looks upwards at them rising towards the sunlight, paving their own path in this world. Up they go until they reach the surface and disappear into the air up above, back to the place where they belong. Luca smiles a stupendously large smile and all the saltwater comes rushing in. She grabs her nose and squints from the burning pain.

It still hurts sometimes; she assumes that to a certain degree it always will. Drowning has its effects even on the ones that survive. She has been submerged for way too long, but at least it gave her the lungs of a swimmer. So there's still hope. After all, these days, no one's a better swimmer than her.

Discover Luna Novella in our store:

https://www.lunapresspublishing.com/shop

CRISIS LINES SUCH AS THESE ARE ESSENTIAL. THEY ALLOW PEOPLE TO REACH OUT WHEN THEY ARE READY TO DO SO.

HTTPS://WWW.THERAPYROUTE.COM/ARTICLE/HELPLINES-SUICIDE-HOTLINES-AND-CRISIS-LINES-FROM-AROUND-THE-WORLD

HTTPS://FINDAHELPLINE.COM/I/IASP

HTTPS://WWW.SUICIDESTOP.COM/CALL_A_HOTLINE.HTML

HTTPS://WWW.SUPPORTLINE.ORG.UK/PROBLEMS/SUICIDE/

HTTPS://WWW.SAMARITANS.ORG/?NATION=SCOTLAND